W.W. JACOBS – THE SHORT STORIES

VOLUME 7

William Wymark Jacobs was born on September 8th, 1863 in the Wapping district of London, England. Jacobs grew up near the docks, where his father was a wharf manager. The docks and river side would be a constant theme of his writing in years to come.

Although surrounded by poverty, he received a formal education in London, first at a private prep school and later at the Birkbeck Literary and Scientific Institute.

His working life began with a less than exciting clerical position at the Post Office Savings Bank. Jacobs put his imagination to good use writing short stories, sketches and articles, many for the Post Office house publication "Blackfriars Magazine."

In 1896 Jacobs published Many Cargoes, a selection of sea-faring yarns, which established him as a popular writer with a knack for authentic dialogue and trick endings.

A year later he published a novelette, The Skipper's Wooing, and in 1898 another collection of short stories; Sea Urchins. These works painted vivid pictures of dockland and seafaring London full of colourful characters.

By 1899, Jacobs was able to quit the post office and write full-time.

He married the noted suffragist Agnes Eleanor Williams (who had been jailed for her protest activities) in 1900. They set up households both in Loughton, Essex and in central London.

The publication in 1902 of At Sunwich Port and Dialstone Lane, in 1904, cemented Jacobs' reputation as one of the leading British authors of the new century.

There followed a string of further successful publications, including Captain's All (1905), Night Watches (1914), The Castaways (1916), and Sea Whispers (1926).

Though Jacobs would create little in the way of new work after 1911, he still wrote and was recognized as a leading humorist, ranked alongside such writers as P. G. Wodehouse.

William Wymark Jacobs died in a North London nursing home in Hornsey Lane, Islington on September 1st, 1943.

Index of Contents

JERRY BUNDLER
KEEPING UP APPEARANCES
KEEPING WATCH
THE LADY OF THE BARGE
LAWYER QUINCE
THE LOST SHIP
LOW WATER
MADE TO MEASURE
THE MADNESS OF MR. LISTER

"MANNERS MAKYTH MAN"
MATED
"MATRIMONIAL OPENINGS"
MIXED RELATIONS
MONEY CHANGERS
THE MONEY-BOX
W.W. JACOBS – A SHORT BIOGRAPHY
W.W. JACOBS – A CONCISE BIBLIOGRAPHY

JERRY BUNDLER

It wanted a few nights to Christmas, a festival for which the small market town of Torchcster was making extensive preparations. The narrow streets which had been thronged with people were now almost deserted; the cheap-jack from London, with the remnant of breath left him after his evening's exertions, was making feeble attempts to blow out his naphtha lamp, and the last shops open were rapidly closing for the night.

In the comfortable coffee-room of the old Boar's Head, half a dozen guests, principally commercial travellers, sat talking by the light of the fire. The talk had drifted from trade to politics, from politics to religion, and so by easy stages to the supernatural. Three ghost stories, never known to fail before, had fallen flat; there was too much noise outside, too much light within. The fourth story was told by an old hand with more success; the streets were quiet, and he had turned the gas out. In the flickering light of the fire, as it shone on the glasses and danced with shadows on the walls, the story proved so enthralling that George, the waiter, whose presence had been forgotten, created a very disagreeable sensation by suddenly starting up from a dark corner and gliding silently from the room. "That's what I call a good story," said one of the men, sipping his hot whisky. "Of course it's an old idea that spirits like to get into the company of human beings. A man told me once that he travelled down the Great Western with a ghost and hadn't the slightest suspicion of it until the inspector came for tickets. My friend said the way that ghost tried to keep up appearances by feeling for it in all its pockets and looking on the floor was quite touching. Ultimately it gave it up and with a faint groan vanished through the ventilator."

"That'll do, Hirst," said another man.

"It's not a subject for jesting," said a little old gentleman who had been an attentive listener. "I've never seen an apparition myself, but I know people who have, and I consider that they form a very interesting link between us and the afterlife. There's a ghost story connected with this house, you know."

"Never heard of it," said another speaker, "and I've been here some years now."

"It dates back a long time now," said the old gentleman. "You've heard about Jerry Bundler, George?"

"Well, I've just 'eard odds and ends, sir," said the old waiter, "but I never put much count to 'em. There was one chap 'ere what said 'e saw it, and the gov'ner sacked 'im prompt."

"My father was a native of this town," said the old gentleman, "and knew the story well. He was a truthful man and a steady churchgoer, but I've heard him declare that once in his life he saw the appearance of Jerry Bundler in this house.".

"And who was this Bundler?" inquired a voice.

"A London thief, pickpocket, highwayman—anything he could turn his dishonest hand to," replied the old gentleman; "and he was run to earth in this house one Christmas week some eighty years ago. He took his last supper in this very room, and after he had gone up to bed a couple of Bow Street runners, who had followed him from London but lost the scent a bit, went upstairs with the landlord and tried the door. It was stout oak, and fast, so one went into the yard, and by means of a short ladder got onto the window-sill, while the other stayed outside the door. Those below in the yard saw the man crouching on the sill, and then there was a sudden smash of glass, and with a cry he fell in a heap on the stones at their feet. Then in the moonlight they saw the white face of the pickpocket peeping over the sill, and while some stayed in the yard, others ran into the house and helped the other man to break the door in. It was difficult to obtain an entrance even then, for it was barred with heavy furniture, but they got in at last, and the first thing that met their eyes was the body of Jerry dangling from the top of the bed by his own handkerchief."

"Which bedroom was it?" asked two or three voices together.

The narrator shook his head. "That I can't tell you; but the story goes that Jerry still haunts this house, and my father used to declare positively that the last time he slept here the ghost of Jerry Bundler lowered itself from the top of his bed and tried to strangle him."

"That'll do," said an uneasy voice. "I wish you'd thought to ask your father which bedroom it was."

"What for?" inquired the old gentleman.

"Well, I should take care not to sleep in it, that's all," said the voice, shortly.

"There's nothing to fear," said the other. "I don't believe for a moment that ghosts could really-hurt one. In fact my father used to confess that it was only the unpleasantness of the thing that upset him, and that for all practical purposes Jerry's fingers might have been made of cottonwool for all the harm they could do."

"That's all very fine," said the last speaker again; "a ghost story is a ghost story, sir; but when a gentleman tells a tale of a ghost in the house in which one is going to sleep, I call it most ungentlemanly!"

"Pooh! nonsense!" said the old gentleman, rising; "ghosts can't hurt you. For my own part, I should rather like to see one. Good night, gentlemen."

"Good night," said the others. "And I only hope Jerry'll pay you a visit," added the nervous man as the door closed.

"Bring some more whisky, George," said a stout commercial; "I want keeping up when the talk turns this way."

"Shall I light the gas, Mr. Malcolm?" said George.

"No; the fire's very comfortable," said the traveller. "Now, gentlemen, any of you know any more?"

"I think we've had enough," said another man; "we shall be thinking we see spirits next, and we're not all like the old gentleman who's just gone."

"Old humbug!" said Hirst. "I should like to put him to the test. Suppose I dress up as Jerry Bundler and go and give him a chance of displaying his courage?"

"Bravo!" said Malcolm, huskily, drowning one or two faint "Noes." "Just for the joke, gentlemen."

"No, no! Drop it, Hirst," said another man.

"Only for the joke," said Hirst, somewhat eagerly. "I've got some things upstairs in which I am going to play in the Rivals—knee-breeches, buckles, and all that sort of thing. It's a rare chance. If you'll wait a bit I'll give you a full-dress rehearsal, entitled, 'Jerry Bundler; or, The Nocturnal Strangler.'"

"You won't frighten us," said the commercial, with a husky laugh.

"I don't know that," said Hirst, sharply; "it's a question of acting, that's all. I'm pretty good, ain't I, Somers?"

"Oh, you're all right—for an amateur," said his friend, with a laugh.

"I'll bet you a level sov. you don't frighten me," said the stout traveller.

"Done!" said Hirst. "I'll take the bet to frighten you first and the old gentleman afterwards. These gentlemen shall be the judges."

"You won't frighten us, sir," said another man, "because we're prepared for you; but you'd better leave the old man alone. It's dangerous play."

"Well, I'll try you first," said Hirst, springing up. "No gas, mind."

He ran lightly upstairs to his room, leaving the others, most of whom had been drinking somewhat freely, to wrangle about his proceedings. It ended in two of them going to bed.

"He's crazy on acting," said Somers, lighting his pipe. "Thinks he's the equal of anybody almost. It doesn't matter with us, but I won't let him go to the old man. And he won't mind so long as he gets an opportunity of acting to us."

"Well, I hope he'll hurry up," said Malcolm, yawning; "it's after twelve now."

Nearly half an hour passed. Malcolm drew his watch from his pocket and was busy winding it, when George, the waiter, who had been sent on an errand to the bar, burst suddenly into the room and rushed towards them.

"'E's comin', gentlemen," he said breathlessly.

"Why, you're frightened, George," said the stout commercial, with a chuckle.

"It was the suddenness of it," said George, sheepishly; "and besides, I didn't look for seein' 'im in the bar. There's only a glimmer of light there, and 'e was sitting on the floor behind the bar. I nearly trod on 'im."

"Oh, you'll never make a man, George," said Malcolm.

"Well, it took me unawares," said the waiter. "Not that I'd have gone to the bar by myself if I'd known 'e was there, and I don't believe you would either, sir."

"Nonsense!" said Malcolm. "I'll go and fetch him in."

"You don't know what it's like, sir," said George, catching him by the sleeve. "It ain't fit to look at by yourself, it ain't, indeed. It's got the—What's that?"

They all started at the sound of a smothered cry from the staircase and the sound of somebody running hurriedly along the passage. Before anybody could speak, the door flew open and a figure bursting into the room flung itself gasping and shivering upon them.

"What is it? What's the matter?" demanded Malcolm. "Why, it's Mr. Hirst." He shook him roughly and then held some spirit to his lips. Hirst drank it greedily and with a sharp intake of his breath gripped him by the arm.

"Light the gas, George," said Malcolm.

The waiter obeyed hastily. Hirst, a ludicrous but pitiable figure in knee-breeches and coat, a large wig all awry and his face a mess of grease paint, clung to him, trembling.

"Now, what's the matter?" asked Malcolm.

"I've seen it," said Hirst, with a hysterical sob. "O Lord, I'll never play the fool again, never!"

"Seen what?" said the others.

"Him—it—the ghost—anything!" said Hirst, wildly.

"Rot!" said Malcolm, uneasily.

"I was coming down the stairs," said Hirst. "Just capering down—as I thought—it ought to do. I felt a tap—"

He broke off suddenly and peered nervously through the open door into the passage.

"I thought I saw it again," he whispered.

"Look—at the foot of the stairs. Can you see anything?"

"No, there's nothing there," said Malcolm, whose own voice shook a little. "Go on. You felt a tap on your shoulder—"

"I turned round and saw it—a little wicked head and a white dead face. Pah!"

"That's what I saw in the bar," said George. "'Orrid it was—devilish!"

Hirst shuddered, and, still retaining his nervous grip of Malcolm's sleeve, dropped into a chair.

"Well, it's a most unaccountable thing," said the dumbfounded Malcolm, turning round to the others. "It's the last time I come to this house."

"I leave to-morrow," said George. "I wouldn't go down to that bar again by myself, no, not for fifty pounds!"

"It's talking about the thing that's caused it, I expect," said one of the men; "we've all been talking about this and having it in our minds. Practically we've been forming a spiritualistic circle without knowing it."

"Hang the old gentleman!" said Malcolm, heartily. "Upon my soul, I'm half afraid to go to bed. It's odd they should both think they saw something."

"I saw it as plain as I see you, sir," said George, solemnly. "P'raps if you keep your eyes turned up the passage you'll see it for yourself."

They followed the direction of his finger, but saw nothing, although one of them fancied that a head peeped round the corner of the wall.

"Who'll come down to the bar?" said Malcolm, looking round.

"You can go, if you like," said one of the others, with a faint laugh; "we'll wait here for you."

The stout traveller walked towards the door and took a few steps up the passage. Then he stopped. All was quite silent, and he walked slowly to the end and looked down fearfully towards the glass partition which shut off the bar. Three times he made as though to go to it; then he turned back, and, glancing over his shoulder, came hurriedly back to the room.

"Did you see it, sir?" whispered George.

"Don't know," said Malcolm, shortly. "I fancied I saw something, but it might have been fancy. I'm in the mood to see anything just now. How are you feeling now, sir?"

"Oh, I feel a bit better now," said Hirst, somewhat brusquely, as all eyes were turned upon him.

"I dare say you think I'm easily scared, but you didn't see it."

"Not at all," said Malcolm, smiling faintly despite himself.

"I'm going to bed," said Hirst, noticing the smile and resenting it. "Will you share my room with me, Somers?"

"I will with pleasure," said his friend, "provided you don't mind sleeping with the gas on full all night."

He rose from his seat, and bidding the company a friendly good-night, left the room with his crestfallen friend. The others saw them to the foot of the stairs, and having heard their door close, returned to the coffee-room.

"Well, I suppose the bet's off?" said the stout commercial, poking the fire and then standing with his legs apart on the hearthrug; "though, as far as I can see, I won it. I never saw a man so scared in all my life. Sort of poetic justice about it, isn't there?"

"Never mind about poetry or justice," said one of his listeners; "who's going to sleep with me?"

"I will," said Malcolm, affably.

"And I suppose we share a room together, Mr. Leek?" said the third man, turning to the fourth.

"No, thank you," said the other, briskly; "I don't believe in ghosts. If anything comes into my room I shall shoot it."

"That won't hurt a spirit, Leek," said Malcolm, decisively.

"Well the noise'll be like company to me," said Leek, "and it'll wake the house too. But if you're nervous, sir," he added, with a grin, to the man who had suggested sharing his room, "George'll be only too pleased to sleep on the door-mat inside your room, I know."

"That I will, sir," said George, fervently; "and if you gentlemen would only come down with me to the bar to put the gas out, I could never be sufficiently grateful."

They went out in a body, with the exception of Leek, peering carefully before them as they went George turned the light out in the bar and they returned unmolested to the coffee-room, and, avoiding the sardonic smile of Leek, prepared to separate for the night.

"Give me the candle while you put the gas out, George," said the traveller.

The waiter handed it to him and extinguished the gas, and at the same moment all distinctly heard a step in the passage outside. It stopped at the door, and as they watched with bated breath, the door creaked and slowly opened. Malcolm fell back open-mouthed, as a white, leering face, with sunken eyeballs and close-cropped bullet head, appeared at the opening.

For a few seconds the creature stood regarding them, blinking in a strange fashion at the candle. Then, with a sidling movement, it came a little way into the room and stood there as if bewildered.

Not a man spoke or moved, but all watched with a horrible fascination as the creature removed its dirty neckcloth and its head rolled on its shoulder. For a minute it paused, and then, holding the rag before it, moved towards Malcolm.

The candle went out suddenly with a flash and a bang. There was a smell of powder, and something writhing n the darkness on the floor. A faint, choking cough, and then silence. Malcolm was the first to speak. "Matches," he said, in a strange voice. George struck one. Then he leapt at the gas and a burner flamed from the match. Malcolm touched the thing on the floor with his foot and found it soft. He looked at his companions. They mouthed inquiries at him, but he shook his head. He lit the candle, and, kneeling down, examined the silent thing on the floor. Then he rose swiftly, and dipping his handkerchief in the water-jug, bent down again and grimly wiped the white face. Then he sprang back with a cry of incredulous horror, pointing at it. Leek's pistol fell to the floor and he shut out the sight with his hands, but the others, crowding forward, gazed spell-bound at the dead face of Hirst.

Before a word was spoken the door opened and Somers hastily entered the room. His eyes fell on the floor. "Good God!" he cried. "You didn't—"

Nobody spoke.

"I told him not to," he said, in a suffocating voice. "I told him not to. I told him—"

He leaned against the wall, deathly sick, put his arms out feebly, and fell fainting into the traveller's arms.

KEEPING UP APPEARANCES

"Everybody is superstitious," said the night-watchman, as he gave utterance to a series of chirruping endearments to a black cat with one eye that had just been using a leg of his trousers as a serviette; "if that cat 'ad stole some men's suppers they'd have acted foolish, and suffered for it all the rest of their lives."

He scratched the cat behind the ear, and despite himself his face darkened. "Slung it over the side, they would," he said, longingly, "and chucked bits o' coke at it till it sank. As I said afore, everybody is superstitious, and those that ain't ought to be night-watchmen for a time—that 'ud cure 'em. I knew one man that killed a black cat, and arter that for the rest of his life he could never get three sheets in the wind without seeing its ghost. Spoilt his life for 'im, it did."

He scratched the cat's other ear. "I only left it a moment, while I went round to the Bull's Head," he said, slowly filling his pipe, "and I thought I'd put it out o' reach. Some men—"

His fingers twined round the animal's neck; then, with a sigh, he rose and took a turn or two on the jetty.

Superstitiousness is right and proper, to a certain extent, he said, resuming his seat; but, o' course, like everything else, some people carry it too far—they'd believe anything. Weak-minded they are, and if you're in no hurry I can tell you a tale of a pal o' mine, Bill Burtenshaw by name, that'll prove my words.

His mother was superstitious afore 'im, and always knew when 'er friends died by hearing three loud taps on the wall. The on'y mistake she ever made was one night when, arter losing no less than seven friends, she found out it was the man next door hanging pictures at three o'clock in the morning. She found it out by 'im hitting 'is thumb-nail.

For the first few years arter he grew up Bill went to sea, and that on'y made 'im more superstitious than ever. Him and a pal named Silas Winch went several v'y'ges together, and their talk used to be that creepy that some o' the chaps was a'most afraid to be left on deck alone of a night. Silas was a long-faced, miserable sort o' chap, always looking on the black side o' things, and shaking his 'ead over it. He thought nothing o' seeing ghosts, and pore old Ben Huggins slept on the floor for a week by reason of a ghost with its throat cut that Silas saw in his bunk. He gave Silas arf a dollar and a neck-tie to change bunks with 'im.

When Bill Burtenshaw left the sea and got married he lost sight of Silas altogether, and the on'y thing he 'ad to remind him of 'im was a piece o' paper which they 'ad both signed with their blood, promising that the fust one that died would appear to the other. Bill agreed to it one evenin' when he didn't know wot he was doing, and for years arterwards 'e used to get the cold creeps down 'is back when he thought of Silas dying fust. And the idea of dying fust 'imself gave 'im cold creeps all over.

Bill was a very good husband when he was sober, but 'is money was two pounds a week, and when a man has all that and on'y a wife to keep out of it, it's natural for 'im to drink. Mrs. Burtenshaw tried all sorts o' ways and means of curing 'im, but it was no use. Bill used to think o' ways, too, knowing the 'arm the drink was doing 'im, and his fav'rite plan was for 'is missis to empty a bucket o' cold water over 'im every time he came 'ome the worse for licker. She did it once, but as she 'ad to spend the rest o' the night in the back yard it wasn't tried again.

Bill got worse as he got older, and even made away with the furniture to get drink with. And then he used to tell 'is missis that he was drove to the pub because his 'ome was so uncomfortable.

Just at that time things was at their worst Silas Winch, who 'appened to be ashore and 'ad got Bill's address from a pal, called to see 'im. It was a Saturday arternoon when he called, and, o' course, Bill was out but 'is missis showed him in, and, arter fetching another chair from the kitchen, asked 'im to sit down.

Silas was very perlite at fust, but arter looking round the room and seeing 'ow bare it was, he gave a little cough, and he ses, "I thought Bill was doing well?" he ses.

"So he is," ses Mrs. Burtenshaw.

Silas Winch coughed again.

"I suppose he likes room to stretch 'imself about in?" he ses, looking round.

Mrs. Burtenshaw wiped 'er eyes and then, knowing 'ow Silas had been an old friend o' Bill's, she drew 'er chair a bit closer and told him 'ow it was. "A better 'usband, when he's sober, you couldn't wish to see," she ses, wiping her eyes agin. "He'd give me anything—if he 'ad it."

Silas's face got longer than ever. "As a matter o' fact," he ses, "I'm a bit down on my luck, and I called round with the 'ope that Bill could lend me a bit, just till I can pull round."

Mrs. Burtenshaw shook her 'ead.

"Well, I s'pose I can stay and see 'im?" ses Silas. "Me and 'im used to be great pals at one time, and many's the good turn I've done him. Wot time'll he be 'ome?"

"Any time after twelve," ses Mrs. Burtenshaw; "but you'd better not be here then. You see, 'im being in that condition, he might think you was your own ghost come according to promise and be frightened out of 'is life. He's often talked about it."

Silas Winch scratched his head and looked at 'er thoughtful-like.

"Why shouldn't he mistake me for a ghost?" he ses at last; "the shock might do 'im good. And, if you come to that, why shouldn't I pretend to be my own ghost and warn 'im off the drink?"

Mrs. Burtenshaw got so excited at the idea she couldn't 'ardly speak, but at last, arter saying over and over agin she wouldn't do such a thing for worlds, she and Silas arranged that he should come in at about three o'clock in the morning and give Bill a solemn warning. She gave 'im her key, and Silas said he'd come in with his 'air and cap all wet and pretend he'd been drowned.

"It's very kind of you to take all this trouble for nothing," ses Mrs. Burtenshaw as Silas got up to go.

"Don't mention it," ses Silas. "It ain't the fust time, and I don't suppose it'll be the last, that I've put myself out to help my feller-creeturs. We all ought to do wot we can for each other."

"Mind, if he finds it out," ses Mrs. Burtenshaw, all of a tremble, "I don't know nothing about it. P'r'aps to make it more life-like I'd better pretend not to see you."

"P'r'aps it would be better," ses Silas, stopping at the street door. "All I ask is that you'll 'ide the poker and anything else that might be laying about handy. And you 'ad better oil the lock so as the key won't make a noise."

Mrs. Burtenshaw shut the door arter 'im, and then she went in and 'ad a quiet sit-down all by 'erself to think it over. The only thing that comforted 'et was that Bill would be in licker, and also that 'e would believe anything in the ghost line.

It was past twelve when a couple o' pals brought him 'ome, and, arter offering to fight all six o' 'em, one after the other, Bill hit the wall for getting in 'is way, and tumbled upstairs to bed. In less than ten minutes 'e was fast asleep, and pore Mrs. Burtenshaw, arter trying her best to keep awake, fell asleep too.

She was woke up suddenly by a noise that froze the marrer in 'er bones— the most 'art-rending groan she 'ad ever heard in 'er life; and, raising her 'ead, she saw Silas Winch standing at the foot of the bed. He 'ad done his face and hands over with wot is called loominous paint, his cap was pushed at the back of his 'ead, and wet wisps of 'air was hanging over his eyes. For a moment Mrs. Burtenshaw's 'art stood still and then Silas let off another groan that put her on edge all over. It was a groan that seemed to come from nothing a'most until it spread into a roar that made the room tremble and rattled the jug in the wash-stand basin. It shook everything in the room but Bill, and he went on sleeping like an infant. Silas did two more groans, and then 'e leaned over the foot o' the bed, and stared at Bill, as though 'e couldn't believe his eyesight.

"Try a squeaky one," ses Mrs. Burtenshaw.

Silas tried five squeaky ones, and then he 'ad a fit o' coughing that would ha' woke the dead, as they say, but it didn't wake Bill.

"Now some more deep ones," ses Mrs. Burtenshaw, in a w'isper.

Silas licked his lips—forgetting the paint—and tried the deep ones agin.

"Now mix 'em a bit," ses Mrs. Burtenshaw.

Silas stared at her. "Look 'ere," he ses, very short, "do you think I'm a fog-horn, or wot?"

He stood there sulky for a moment, and then 'e invented a noise that nothing living could miss hearing; even Bill couldn't. He moved in 'is sleep, and arter Silas 'ad done it twice more he turned and spoke to 'is missis about it. "D'ye hear?" he ses; "stop it. Stop it at once."

Mrs. Burtenshaw pretended to be asleep, and Bill was just going to turn over agin when Silas let off another groan. It was on'y a little one this time, but Bill sat up as though he 'ad been shot, and he no sooner caught sight of Silas standing there than 'e gave a dreadful 'owl and, rolling over, wropped 'imself up in all the bed-clothes 'e could lay his 'ands on. Then Mrs. Burtenshaw gave a 'owl and tried to get some of 'em back; but Bill, thinking it was the ghost, only held on tighter than ever.

"Bill!" ses Silas Winch, in an awful voice.

Bill gave a kick, and tried to bore a hole through the bed.

"Bill," ses Silas agin, "why don't you answer me? I've come all the way from the bottom of the Pacific Ocean to see you, and this is all I get for it. Haven't you got anything to say to me?"

"Good-by," ses Bill, in a voice all smothered with the bed-clothes.

Silas Winch groaned agin, and Bill, as the shock 'ad made a'most sober, trembled all over.

"The moment I died," ses Silas, "I thought of my promise towards you. 'Bill's expecting me,' I ses, and, instead of staying in comfort at the bottom of the sea, I kicked off the body of the cabin-boy wot was clinging round my leg, and 'ere I am."

"It was very—t-t-thoughtful—of you—Silas," ses Bill; "but you always— w-w-was—thoughtful. Good-by—"

Afore Silas could answer, Mrs. Burtenshaw, who felt more comfortable, 'aving got a bit o' the clothes back, thought it was time to put 'er spoke in.

"Lor' bless me, Bill," she ses. "Wotever are you a-talking to yourself like this for? 'Ave you been dreaming?"

"Dreaming!" ses pore Bill, catching hold of her 'and and gripping it till she nearly screamed. "I wish I was. Can't you see it?"

"See it?" ses his wife. "See wot?"

"The ghost," ses Bill, in a 'orrible whisper; "the ghost of my dear, kind old pal, Silas Winch. The best and noblest pal a man ever 'ad. The kindest-'arted—"

"Rubbish," ses Mrs. Burtenshaw. "You've been dreaming. And as for the kindest-'arted pal, why I've often heard you say—"

"H'sh!" ses Bill. "I didn't. I'll swear I didn't. I never thought of such a thing."

"You turn over and go to sleep," ses his wife, "hiding your 'ead under the clothes like a child that's afraid o' the dark! There's nothing there, I tell you. Wot next will you see, I wonder? Last time it was a pink rat."

"This is fifty million times worse than pink rats," ses Bill. "I on'y wish it was a pink rat."

"I tell you there is nothing there," ses his wife. "Look!"

Bill put his 'ead up and looked, and then 'e gave a dreadful scream and dived under the bed-clothes agin.

"Oh, well, 'ave it your own way, then," ses his wife. "If it pleases you to think there is a ghost there, and to go on talking to it, do so, and welcome."

She turned over and pretended to go to sleep agin, and arter a minute or two Silas spoke agin in the same hollow voice.

"Bill!" he ses.

"Yes," ses Bill, with a groan of his own.

"She can't see me," ses Silas, "and she can't 'ear me; but I'm 'ere all right. Look!"

"I 'ave looked," ses Bill, with his 'ead still under the clothes.

"We was always pals, Bill, you and me," ses Silas; "many a v'y'ge 'ave we had together, mate, and now I'm a-laying at the bottom of the Pacific Ocean, and you are snug and 'appy in your own warm bed. I 'ad to come to see you, according to promise, and over and above that, since I was drowned my eyes 'ave been opened. Bill, you're drinking yourself to death!"

"I—I—didn't know it," ses Bill, shaking all over. "I'll knock it—off a bit, and—thank you—for—w-w-warning me. G-G-Good-by."

"You'll knock it off altogether," ses Silas Winch, in a awful voice. "You're not to touch another drop of beer, wine, or spirits as long as you live. D'ye hear me?"

"Not—not as medicine?" ses Bill, holding the clothes up a bit so as to be more distinct.

"Not as anything," ses Silas; "not even over Christmas pudding. Raise your right arm above your 'ead and swear by the ghost of pore Silas Winch, as is laying at the bottom of the Pacific Ocean, that you won't touch another drop."

Bill Burtenshaw put 'is arm up and swore it.

Then 'e took 'is arm in agin and lay there wondering wot was going to 'appen next.

"If you ever break your oath by on'y so much as a teaspoonful," ses Silas, "you'll see me agin, and the second time you see me you'll die as if struck by lightning. No man can see me twice and live."

Bill broke out in a cold perspiration all over. "You'll be careful, won't you, Silas?" he ses. "You'll remember you 'ave seen me once, I mean?"

"And there's another thing afore I go," ses Silas. "I've left a widder, and if she don't get 'elp from some one she'll starve."

"Pore thing," ses Bill. "Pore thing."

"If you 'ad died afore me," ses Silas, "I should 'ave looked arter your good wife—wot I've now put in a sound sleep—as long as I lived."

Bill didn't say anything.

"I should 'ave given 'er fifteen shillings a week," ses Silas.

"'Ow much?" ses Bill, nearly putting his 'ead up over the clothes, while 'is wife almost woke up with surprise and anger.

"Fifteen shillings," ses Silas, in 'is most awful voice. "You'll save that over the drink."

"I—I'll go round and see her," ses Bill. "S'he might be one o' these 'ere independent—" 277

"I forbid you to go near the place," ses Silas. "Send it by post every week; 15 Shap Street will find her. Put your arm up and swear it; same as you did afore."

Bill did as 'e was told, and then 'e lay and trembled, as Silas gave three more awful groans.

"Farewell, Bill," he ses. "Farewell. I am going back to my bed at the bottom o' the sea. So long as you keep both your oaths I shall stay there. If you break one of 'em or go to see my pore wife I shall appear agin. Farewell! Farewell! Farewell!"

Bill said "Good-by," and arter a long silence he ventured to put an eye over the edge of the clothes and discovered that the ghost 'ad gone. He lay awake for a couple o' hours, wondering and saying over the address to himself so that he shouldn't forget it, and just afore it was time to get up he fell into a peaceful slumber. His wife didn't get a wink, and she lay there trembling with passion to think 'ow she'd been done, and wondering 'ow she was to alter it.

Bill told 'er all about it in the morning; and then with tears in his eyes 'e went downstairs and emptied a little barrel o' beer down the sink. For the fust two or three days 'e went about with a thirst that he'd ha' given pounds for if 'e'd been allowed to satisfy it, but arter a time it went off, and then, like all teetotallers, 'e began to run down drink and call it pison.

The fust thing 'e did when 'e got his money on Friday was to send off a post-office order to Shap Street, and Mrs. Burtenshaw cried with rage and 'ad to put it down to the headache. She 'ad the headache every Friday for a month, and Bill, wot was feeling stronger and better than he 'ad done for years, felt quite sorry for her.

By the time Bill 'ad sent off six orders she was worn to skin and bone a'most a-worrying over the way Silas Winch was spending her money. She dursn't undeceive Bill for two reasons: fust of all, because she didn't want 'im to take to drink again; and secondly, for fear of wot he might do to 'er if 'e found out 'ow she'd been deceiving 'im.

She was laying awake thinking it over one night while Bill was sleeping peaceful by her side, when all of a sudden she 'ad an idea. The more she thought of it the better it seemed; but she laid awake for ever so long afore she dared to do more than think. Three or four times she turned and looked at Bill and listened to 'im breathing, and then, trembling all over with fear and excitement, she began 'er little game.

"He did send it," she ses, with a piercing scream. "He did send it."

"W-w-wot's the matter?" ses Bill, beginning to wake up.

Mrs. Burtenshaw didn't take any notice of 'im.

"He did send it," she ses, screaming agin. "Every Friday night reg'lar. Oh, don't let 'im see you agin."

Bill, wot was just going to ask 'er whether she 'ad gone mad, gave a awful 'owl and disappeared right down in the middle o' the bed.

"There's some mistake," ses Mrs. Burtenshaw, in a voice that could ha' been 'eard through arf-a-dozen beds easy. "It must ha' been lost in the post. It must ha' been."

She was silent for a few seconds, then she ses, "All right," she ses, "I'll bring it myself, then, by hand every week. No, Bill sha'n't come; I'll promise that for 'im. Do go away; he might put his 'ead up at any moment."

She began to gasp and sob, and Bill began to think wot a good wife he 'ad got, when he felt 'er put a couple of pillers over where she judged his 'ead to be, and hold 'em down with her arm.

"Thank you, Mr. Winch," she ses, very loud. "Thank you. Good-by, Good-by."

She began to quieten down a bit, although little sobs, like wimmen use when they pretend that they want to leave off crying but can't, kept breaking out of 'er. Then, by and by, she quieted down altogether and a husky voice from near the foot of the bed ses: "Has it gorn?"

"Oh, Bill," she ses, with another sob, "I've seen the ghost!"

"Has it gorn?" ses Bill, agin.

"Yes, it's gorn," ses his wife, shivering. "Oh, Bill, it stood at the foot of the bed looking at me, with its face and 'ands all shiny white, and damp curls on its forehead. Oh!"

Bill came up very slow and careful, but with 'is eyes still shut.

"His wife didn't get the money this week," ses Mrs. Burtenshaw; "but as he thought there might be a mistake somewhere he appeared to me instead of to you. I've got to take the money by hand."

"Yes, I heard," ses Bill; "and mind, if you should lose it or be robbed of it, let me know at once. D'ye hear? At once!"

"Yes, Bill," ses 'is wife.

They lay quiet for some time, although Mrs. Burtenshaw still kept trembling and shaking; and then Bill ses. "Next time a man tells you he 'as seen a ghost, p'r'aps you'll believe in 'im."

Mrs. Burtenshaw took out the end of the sheet wot she 'ad stuffed in 'er mouth when 'e began to speak.

"Yes, Bill," she ses.

Bill Burtenshaw gave 'er the fifteen shillings next morning and every Friday night arterwards; and that's 'ow it is that, while other wimmen 'as to be satisfied looking at new hats and clothes in the shop-winders, Mrs. Burtenshaw is able to wear 'em.

KEEPING WATCH

"Human natur'!" said the night-watchman, gazing fixedly at a pretty girl in a passing waterman's skiff. "Human natur'!"

He sighed, and, striking a match, applied it to his pipe and sat smoking thoughtfully.

"The young fellow is pretending that his arm is at the back of her by accident," he continued; "and she's pretending not to know that it's there. When he's allowed to put it round 'er waist whenever he wishes, he won't want to do it. She's artful enough to know that, and that's why they are all so stand-offish until the thing is settled. She'll move forward 'arf an inch presently, and 'arf a minute arterwards she'll lean back agin without thinking. She's a nice-looking gal, and what she can see in a tailor's dummy like that, I can't think."

He leaned back on his box and, folding his arms, emitted a cloud of smoke.

"Human natur's a funny thing. I've seen a lot of it in my time, and if I was to 'ave my life all over agin I expect I should be just as silly as them two in the skiff. I've known the time when I would spend money as free over a gal as I would over myself. I on'y wish I'd got all the money now that I've spent on peppermint lozenges.

"That gal in the boat reminds me o' one I used to know a few years ago. Just the same innercent baby look—a look as if butter wouldn't melt in 'er mouth—and a artful disposition that made me sorry for 'er sects.

"She used to come up to this wharf once a week in a schooner called the Belle. Her father, Cap'n Butt, was a widow-man, and 'e used to bring her with 'im, partly for company and partly because 'e could keep 'is eye on her. Nasty eye it, was, too, when he 'appened to be out o' temper.

"I'd often took a bit o' notice o' the gal; just giving 'er a kind smile now and then as she sat on deck, and sometimes—when 'er father wasn't looking—she'd smile back. Once, when 'e was down below, she laughed right out. She was afraid of 'im, and by and by I noticed that she daren't even get off the ship and walk up and down the wharf without asking 'im. When she went out 'e was with 'er, and, from one or two nasty little snacks I 'appened to overhear when the skipper thought I was too far away, I began to see that something was up.

"It all came out one evening, and it only came out because the skipper wanted my help. I was standing leaning on my broom to get my breath back arter a bit o' sweeping, when he came up to me, and I knew at once, by the nice way 'e spoke, that he wanted me to do something for 'im.

"'Come and 'ave a pint, Bill,' he ses.

"I put my broom agin the wall, and we walked round to the Bull's Head like a couple o' brothers. We 'ad two pints apiece, and then he put his 'and on my shoulder and talked as man to man.

"'I'm in a little bit o' difficulty about that gal o' mine,' he ses, passing me his baccy-box. 'Six months ago she dropped a letter out of 'er pocket, and I'm blest if it wasn't from a young man. A young man!'

"'You sur-prise me,' I ses, meaning to be sarcastic.

"'I surprised her,' he ses, looking very fierce. 'I went to 'er box and I found a pile of 'em-a pile of 'em-tied up with a piece o' pink ribbon. And a photygraph of my lord. And of all the narrer-chested, weak-eyed, slack-baked, spindly-legged sons of a gun you ever saw in your life, he is the worst. If I on'y get my 'ands on him I'll choke 'im with his own feet.'

"He washed 'is mouth out with a drop o' beer and stood scowling at the floor.

"'Arter I've choked 'im I'll twist his neck,' he ses. 'If he 'ad on'y put his address on 'is letters, I'd go round and do it now. And my daughter, my only daughter, won't tell me where he lives.'

"'She ought to know better,' I ses.

"He took hold o' my 'and and shook it. 'You've got more sense than one 'ud think to look at you, Bill,' he ses, not thinking wot he was saying. 'You see wot a mess I'm in.'

"'Yes,' I ses.

"'I'm a nurse, that's wot I am,' he ses, very savage. 'Just a nursemaid. I can't move 'and or foot without that gal. 'Ow'd you like it, yourself, Bill?'

"'It must be very orkard for you,' I ses. 'Very orkard indeed.'

"'Orkard !' he ses; 'it's no name for it, Bill. I might as well be a Sunday-school teacher, and ha' done with it. I never 'ad such a dull time in all my life. Never. And the worst of it is, it's spiling my temper. And all because o' that narrer-eyed, red-chested—you know wot I mean!'

"He took another mouthful o' beer, and then he took 'old of my arm. 'Bill,' he ses, very earnest, 'I want you to do me a favour.'

"'Go ahead,' I ses.

"'I've got to meet a pal at Charing Cross at ha'-past seven,' he ses; 'and we're going to make a night of it. I've left Winnie in charge o' the cook, and I've told 'im plain that, if she ain't there when I come back, I'll skin 'im alive. Now, I want you to watch 'er, too. Keep the gate locked, and don't let anybody in you don't know. Especially that monkey-faced imitation of a man. Here 'e is. That's his likeness.'

"He pulled a photygraph out of 'is coatpocket and 'anded it to me.

"'That's 'im,' he ses. 'Fancy a gal getting love-letters from a thing like that! And she was on'y twenty last birthday. Keep your eye on 'er, Bill, and don't let 'er out of your sight. You're worth two o' the cook.'

"He finished 'is beer, and, cuddling my arm, stepped back to the wharf. Miss Butt was sitting on the cabin skylight reading a book, and old Joe, the cook, was standing near 'er pretending to swab the decks with a mop.

"'I've got to go out for a little while—on business,' ses the skipper. 'I don't s'pose I shall be long, and, while I'm away, Bill and the cook will look arter you.'

"Miss Butt wrinkled up 'er shoulders.

"'The gate'll be locked, and you're not to leave the wharf. D'ye 'ear?'

"The gal wriggled 'er shoulders agin and went on reading, but she gave the cook a look out of 'er innercent baby eyes that nearly made 'im drop the mop.

"'Them's my orders,' ses the skipper, swelling his chest and looking round, 'to everybody. You know wot'll 'appen to you, Joe, if things ain't right when I come back. Come along, Bill, and lock the gate arter me. An' mind, for your own sake, don't let anything 'appen to that gal while I'm away.'

"'Wot time'll you be back?' I ses, as 'e stepped through the wicket.

"'Not afore twelve, and p'r'aps a good bit later,' he ses, smiling all over with 'appiness. 'But young slab-chest don't know I'm out, and Winnie thinks I'm just going out for 'arf an hour, so it'll be all right. So long.'

"I watched 'im up the road, and I must say I began to wish I 'adn't taken the job on. Arter all, I 'ad on'y had two pints and a bit o' flattery, and I knew wot 'ud 'appen if anything went wrong. Built like a bull he was, and fond o' using his strength. I locked the wicket careful, and, putting the key in my pocket, began to walk up and down the wharf.

"For about ten minutes the gal went on reading and didn't look up once. Then, as I passed, she gave me a nice smile and shook 'er little fist at the cook, wot 'ad got 'is back towards 'er. I smiled back, o' course, and by and by she put her book down and climbed on to the side o' the ship and held out her 'and for me to 'elp her ashore.

"'I'm so tired of the ship,' she ses, in a soft voice; 'it's like a prison. Don't you get, tired of the wharf?'

"'Sometimes,' I ses; 'but it's my dooty.'

"'Yes,' she ses. 'Yes, of course. But you're a big, strong man, and you can put up with things better.'

"She gave a little sigh, and we walked up and down for a time without saying anything.

"'And it's all father's foolishness,' she ses, at last; 'that's wot makes it so tiresome. I can't help a pack of silly young men writing to me, can I?'

"'No, I s'pose not,' I ses.

"'Thank you,' she ses, putting 'er little 'and on my arm. 'I knew that you were sensible. I've often watched you when I've been sitting alone on the schooner, longing for somebody to speak to. And I'm a good judge of character. I can read you like a book.'

"She turned and looked up at me. Beautiful blue eyes she'd got, with long, curling lashes, and teeth like pearls.

"'Father is so silly,' she ses, shaking her 'ead and looking down; 'and it's so unreasonable, because, as a matter of fact, I don't like young men. Oh, I beg your pardon, I didn't mean that. I didn't mean to be rude.'

"'Rude?' I ses, staring at her.

"'Of course it was a rude thing for me to say,' she ses, smiling; 'because you are still a young man yourself.'

"I shook my 'ead. 'Youngish,' I ses.

"'Young!' she ses, stamping 'er little foot.

"She gave me another look, and this time 'er blue eyes seemed large and solemn. She walked along like one in a dream, and twice she tripped over the planks and would 'ave fallen if I hadn't caught 'er round the waist.

"'Thank you,' she ses. 'I'm very clumsy. How strong your arm is!'

"We walked up and down agin, and every time we went near the edge of the jetty she 'eld on to my arm for fear of stumbling agin. And there was that silly cook standing about on the schooner on tip-toe and twisting his silly old neck till I wonder it didn't twist off.

"'Wot a beautiful evening it is!' she ses, at last, in a low voice. 'I 'ope father isn't coming back early. Do you know wot time he is coming home?'

"'About twelve,' I ses; 'but don't tell 'im I told you so.'

"'O' course not,' she ses, squeezing my arm. 'Poor father! I hope he is enjoying himself as much as I am.'

"We walked down to the jetty agin arter that, and sat side by side looking acrost the river. And she began to talk about Life, and wot a strange thing it was; and 'ow the river would go on flowing down to the sea thousands and thousands o' years arter we was both dead and forgotten. If it hadn't ha' been for her little 'ead leaning agin my shoulder I should have 'ad the creeps.

"'Let's go down into the cabin,' she ses, at last, with a little shiver; 'it makes me melancholy sitting here and thinking of the "might-have-beens."'

"I got up first and 'elped her up, and, arter both staring hard at the cook, wot didn't seem to know 'is place, we went down into the cabin. It was a comfortable little place, and arter she 'ad poured me out a glass of 'er father's whisky, and filled my pipe for me, I wouldn't ha' changed places with a king. Even when the pipe wouldn't draw I didn't mind.

"'May I write a letter?' she ses, at last.

"'Sartainly,' I ses.

"She got out her pen and ink and paper, and wrote. 'I sha'n't be long,' she ses, looking up and nibbling 'er pen. 'It's a letter to my dressmaker; she promised my dress by six o'clock this afternoon, and I am just writing to tell her that if I don't have it by ten in the morning she can keep it.'

"'Quite right,' I ses; 'it's the on'y way to get things done.'

"'It's my way,' she ses, sticking the letter in an envelope and licking it down. 'Nice name, isn't it?'

"She passed it over to me, and I read the name and address: 'Miss Minnie Miller, 17, John Street, Mile End Road.'

"'That'll wake her up,' She ses, smiling. 'Will you ask Joe to take it for me?'

"'He—he's on guard,' I ses, smiling back at 'er and shaking my 'ead.

"'I know,' she ses, in a low voice. 'But I don't want any guard—only you. I don't like guards that peep down skylights.'

"I looked up just in time to see Joe's 'ead disappear. Then I nipped up, and arter I 'ad told 'im part of wot I thought about 'im I gave 'im the letter and told 'im to sheer off.

"'The skipper told me to stay 'ere,' he ses, looking obstinate.

"'You do as you're told,' I ses. 'I'm in charge, and I take full responsibility. I shall lock the gate arter you. Wot are you worrying about?'

"'And here's a shilling, Joe, for a bus fare,' ses the gal, smiling. 'You can keep the change.'

"Joe took off 'is cap and scratched 'is silly bald 'ead.

"'Come on,' I ses; 'it's a letter to a dressmaker. A letter that must go to-night.'

"'Else it's no use,' ses the gal. 'You don't know 'ow important it is.'

"'All right,' ses Joe. ''Ave it your own way. So long as you don't tell the skipper I don't mind. If anything 'appens you'll catch it too, Bill.'

"He climbed ashore, and I follered 'im to the gate and unlocked it. He was screwing up 'is eye ready for a wink, but I give 'im such a look that he thought better of it, and, arter rubbing his eye with 'is finger as though he 'ad got a bit o' dust in it, he went off.

"I locked the gate and went back to the cabin, and for some time we sat talking about fathers and the foolish ideas they got into their 'eads, and things o' that sort. So far as I remember, I 'ad two more goes o' whisky and one o' the skipper's cigars, and I was just thinking wot a beautiful thing it was to be alive and 'ealthy and in good spirits, talking to a nice gal that understood wot you said a'most afore you said it, when I 'eard three blows on a whistle.

"'Wot's that?' I ses, starting up. 'Police whistle?'

"'I don't think so,' ses Miss Butt, putting her 'and on my shoulder. 'Sit down and stay where you are. I don't want you to get hurt, if it is. Let somebody I don't like go.'

"I sat down agin and listened, but there was no more whistling.

"'Boy in the street, I expect,' ses the gal, going into the state-room. 'Oh, I've got something to show you. Wait a minute.'

"I 'eard her moving about, and then she comes back into the cabin.

"'I can't find the key of my box,' she ses, 'and it's in there. I wonder whether you've got a key that would open it. It's a padlock.'

"I put my 'and in my pocket and pulled out my keys. 'Shall I come and try?' I ses.

"'No, thank you,' she ses, taking the keys. 'This looks about the size. What key is it?'

"'It's the key of the gate,' I ses, 'but I don't suppose it'll fit.'

"She went back into the state-room agin, and I 'eard her fumbling at a lock. Then she came back into the cabin, breathing rather hard, and stood thinking.

"'I've just remembered,' she ses, pinching her chin. 'Yes!'

"She stepped to the door and went up the companion-ladder, and the next moment I 'eard a sliding noise and a key turn in a lock. I jumped to the foot of the ladder and, 'ardly able to believe my senses, saw that the hatch was closed. When I found that it was locked too, you might ha' knocked me down with a feather.

"I went down to the cabin agin, and, standing on the locker, pushed the skylight up with my 'ead and tried to lookout. I couldn't see the gate, but I 'eard voices and footsteps, and a little while arterwards I see that gal coming along the wharf arm in arm with the young man she 'ad told me she didn't like, and dancing for joy. They climbed on to the schooner, and then they both stooped down with their hands on their knees and looked at me.

"'Wot is it?' ses the young man, grinning.

"'It's a watchman,' ses the gal. 'It's here to take charge of the wharf, you know, and see that nobody comes on.'

"'We ought to ha' brought some buns for it,' ses the young man; 'look at it opening its mouth.'

"They both laughed fit to kill themselves, but I didn't move a muscle.

"'You open the companion,' I ses, 'or it'll be the worse for you. D'ye hear? Open it !'

"'Oh, Alfred,' ses the gal, 'he's losing 'is temper. Wotever shall we do?'

"'I don't want no more nonsense,' I ses, trying to fix 'er with my eye. 'If you don't let me out it'll be the worse for you.'

"'Don't you talk to my young lady like that,' ses the young man.

"'Your young lady?' I ses. 'H'mm! You should ha' seen 'er 'arf an hour ago.'

"The gal looked at me steady for a moment.

"'He put 'is nasty fat arm round my waist, Alfred,' she ses.

"'Wot!' ses the young man, squeaking. 'WOT!'

"He snatched up the mop wot that nasty, untidy cook 'ad left leaning agin the side, and afore I 'ad any idea of wot 'e was up to he shoved the beastly thing straight in my face.

"'Next time,' he ses, 'I'll tear you limb from limb!'

"I couldn't speak for a time, and when I could 'e stopped me with the mop agin. It was like a chained lion being tormented by a monkey. I stepped down on to the cabin floor, and then I told 'em both wot I thought of 'em.

"'Come along, Alfred,' ses the gal, 'else the cook'll be back before we start.'

"'He's all right,' ses the young man. 'Minnie's looking arter him. When I left he'd got 'arf a bottle of whisky in front of 'im.'

"'Still, we may as well go,' ses Miss Butt. 'It seems a shame to keep the cab waiting.'

"'All right,' he ses. 'I just want to give this old chump one more lick with the mop and then we'll go.'

"He peeped down the skylight and waited, but I kept quite quiet, with my back towards 'im.

"'Come along,' ses Miss Butt.

"'I'm coming,' he ses. 'Hi! You down there! When the cap'n comes back tell 'im that I'm taking Miss Butt to an aunt o' mine in the country. And tell 'im that in a week or two he'll 'ave the largest and nicest piece of wedding-cake he 'as ever 'ad in his life. So long!'

"'Good-bye, watchman,' ses the gal.

"They moved off without another word—from them, I mean. I heard the wicket slam and then I 'eard a cab drive off over the stones. I couldn't believe it at first. I couldn't believe a gal with such beautiful blue eyes could be so hard-'earted, and for a long time I stood listening and hoping to 'ear the cab come back. Then I stepped up to the companion and tried to shift it with my shoulders.

"I went back to the cabin at last, and arter lighting the lamp I 'ad another sup o' the skipper's whisky to clear my 'ead, and sat down to try and think wot tale I was to tell 'im. I sat for pretty near three hours without thinking of one, and then I 'eard the crew come on to the wharf.

"They was a bit startled when they saw my 'ead at the skylight, and then they all started at the same time asking me wot I was doing. I told 'em to let me out fust and then I'd tell 'em, and one of 'em 'ad just stepped round to the companion when the skipper come on to the wharf and stepped aboard. He stooped down and peeped at me through the skylight as though he couldn't believe 'is eyesight, and then, arter sending the hands for'ard and telling 'em to stay there, wotever 'appened, he unlocked the companion and came down."

THE LADY OF THE BARGE

The master of the barge Arabella sat in the stern of his craft with his right arm leaning on the tiller. A desultory conversation with the mate of a schooner, who was hanging over the side of his craft a few yards off, had come to a conclusion owing to a difference of opinion on the subject of religion. The skipper had argued so warmly that he almost fancied he must have inherited the tenets of the Seventh-day Baptists from his mother while the mate had surprised himself by the warmth of his advocacy of a form of Wesleyanism which would have made the members of that sect open their eyes with horror. He had, moreover, confirmed the skipper in the error of his ways by calling him a bargee, the ranks of the Baptists receiving a defender if not a recruit from that hour.

With the influence of the religious argument still upon him, the skipper, as the long summer's day gave place to night, fell to wondering where his own mate, who was also his brother-in-law, had got to. Lights which had been struggling with the twilight now burnt bright and strong, and the skipper, moving from the shadow to where a band of light fell across the deck, took out a worn silver watch and saw that it was ten o'clock.

Almost at the same moment a dark figure appeared on the jetty above and began to descend the ladder, and a strongly built young man of twenty-two sprang nimbly to the deck.

"Ten o'clock, Ted," said the skipper, slowly. "It 'll be eleven in an hour's time," said the mate, calmly.

"That 'll do," said the skipper, in a somewhat loud voice, as he noticed that his late adversary still occupied his favourite strained position, and a fortuitous expression of his mother's occurred to him: "Don't talk to me; I've been arguing with a son of Belial for the last half-hour."

"Bargee," said the son of Belial, in a dispassionate voice.

"Don't take no notice of him, Ted," said the skipper, pityingly.

"He wasn't talking to me," said Ted. "But never mind about him; I want to speak to you in private."

"Fire away, my lad," said the other, in a patronizing voice.

"Speak up," said the voice from the schooner, encouragingly. "I'm listening."

There was no reply from the bargee. The master led the way to the cabin, and lighting a lamp, which appealed to more senses than one, took a seat on a locker, and again requested the other to fire away.

"Well, you see, it's this way," began the mate, with a preliminary wriggle: "there's a certain young woman—"

"A certain young what?" shouted the master of the Arabella.

"Woman," repeated the mate, snappishly; "you've heard of a woman afore, haven't you? Well, there's a certain young woman I'm walking out with I—"

"Walking out?" gasped the skipper. "Why, I never 'eard o' such a thing."

"You would ha' done if you'd been better looking, p'raps," retorted the other. "Well, I've offered this young woman to come for a trip with us."

"Oh, you have, 'ave you!" said the skipper, sharply. "And what do you think Louisa will say to it?"

"That's your look out," said Louisa's brother, cheerfully. "I'll make her up a bed for'ard, and we'll all be as happy as you please."

He started suddenly. The mate of the schooner was indulging in a series of whistles of the most amatory description.

"There she is," he said. "I told her to wait outside."

He ran upon deck, and his perturbed brother-in-law, following at his leisure, was just in time to see him descending the ladder with a young woman and a small handbag.

"This is my brother-in-law, Cap'n Gibbs," said Ted, introducing the new arrival; "smartest man at a barge on the river."

The girl extended a neatly gloved hand, shook the skipper's affably, and looked wonderingly about her.

"It's very close to the water, Ted," she said, dubiously.

The skipper coughed. "We don't take passengers as a rule," he said, awkwardly; "we 'ain't got much convenience for them."

"Never mind," said the girl, kindly; "I sha'nt expect too much."

She turned away, and following the mate down to the cabin, went into ecstasies over the space-saving contrivances she found there. The drawers fitted in the skipper's bunk were a source of particular interest, and the owner watched with strong disapprobation through the skylight her efforts to make him an apple-pie bed with the limited means at her disposal. He went down below at once as a wet blanket.

"I was just shaking your bed up a bit," said Miss Harris, reddening.

"I see you was," said the skipper, briefly.

He tried to pluck up courage to tell her that he couldn't take her, but only succeeded in giving vent to an inhospitable cough.

"I'll get the supper," said the mate, suddenly; "you sit down, old man, and talk to Lucy."

In honour of the visitor he spread a small cloth, and then proceeded to produce cold beef, pickles, and accessories in a manner which reminded Miss Harris of white rabbits from a conjurer's hat. Captain Gibbs, accepting the inevitable, ate his supper in silence and left them to their glances.

"We must make you up a bed, for'ard, Lucy," said the mate, when they had finished.

Miss Harris started. "Where's that?" she inquired.

"Other end o' the boat," replied the mate, gathering up some bedding under his arm. "You might bring a lantern, John."

The skipper, who was feeling more sociable after a couple of glasses of beer, complied, and accompanied the couple to the tiny forecastle. A smell compounded of bilge, tar, paint, and other healthy disinfectants emerged as the scuttle was pushed back. The skipper dangled the lantern down and almost smiled.

"I can't sleep there," said the girl, with decision. "I shall die o' fright."

"You'll get used to it," said Ted, encouragingly, as he helped her down; "it's quite dry and comfortable."

He put his arm round her waist and squeezed her hand, and aided by this moral support, Miss Harris not only consented to remain, but found various advantages in the forecastle over the cabin, which had escaped the notice of previous voyagers.

"I'll leave you the lantern," said the mate, making it fast, "and we shall be on deck most o' the night. We get under way at two."

He quitted the forecastle, followed by the skipper, after a polite but futile attempt to give him precedence, and made his way to the cabin for two or three hours' sleep.

"There'll be a row at the other end, Ted," said the skipper, nervously, as he got into his bunk. "Louisa's sure to blame me for letting you keep company with a gal like this. We was talking about you only the other day, and she said if you was married five years from now, it 'ud be quite soon enough."

"Let Loo mind her own business," said the mate, sharply; "she's not going to nag me. She's not my wife, thank goodness!"

He turned over and fell fast asleep, waking up fresh and bright three hours later, to commence what he fondly thought would be the pleasantest voyage of his life.

The Arabella dropped slowly down with the tide, the wind being so light that she was becalmed by every tall warehouse on the way. Off Greenwich, however, the breeze freshened somewhat, and a little later Miss Harris, looking somewhat pale as to complexion and untidy as to hair, came slowly on deck.

"Where's the looking-glass?" she asked, as Ted hastened to greet her. "How does my hair look?"

"All wavy," said the infatuated young man; "all little curls and squiggles. Come down in the cabin; there's a glass there."

Miss Harris, with a light nod to the skipper as he sat at the tiller, followed the mate below, and giving vent to a little cry of indignation as she saw herself in the glass, waved the amorous Ted on deck, and started work on her disarranged hair.

At breakfast-time a little friction was caused by what the mate bitterly termed the narrow-minded, old-fashioned ways of the skipper. He had arranged that the skipper should steer while he and Miss Harris breakfasted, but the coffee was no sooner on the table than the skipper called him, and relinquishing the helm in his favour, went below to do the honours. The mate protested.

"It's not proper," said the skipper. "Me and 'er will 'ave our meals together, and then you must have yours. She's under my care."

Miss Harris assented blithely, and talk and laughter greeted the ears of the indignant mate as he steered. He went down at last to cold coffee and lukewarm herrings, returning to the deck after a hurried meal to find the skipper narrating some of his choicest experiences to an audience which hung on his lightest word.

The disregard they showed for his feelings was maddening, and for the first time in his life he became a prey to jealousy in its worst form. It was quite clear to him that the girl had become desperately enamoured of the skipper, and he racked his brain in a wild effort to discover the reason.

With an idea of reminding his brother-in-law of his position, he alluded two or three times in a casual fashion to his wife. The skipper hardly listened to him, and patting Miss Harris's cheek in a fatherly manner, regaled her with an anecdote of the mate's boyhood which the latter had spent a goodly portion of his life in denying. He denied it again, hotly, and Miss Harris, conquering for a time her laughter, reprimanded him severely for contradicting.

By the time dinner was ready he was in a state of sullen apathy, and when the meal was over and the couple came on deck again, so far forgot himself as to compliment Miss Harris upon her appetite.

"I'm ashamed of you, Ted," said the skipper, with severity.

"I'm glad you know what shame is," retorted the mate.

"If you can't be'ave yourself, you'd better keep a bit for'ard till you get in a better temper," continued the skipper.

"I'll be pleased to," said the smarting mate. "I wish the barge was longer."

"It couldn't be too long for me," said Miss Harris, tossing her head.

"Be'aving like a schoolboy," murmured the skipper.

"I know how to behave *my*-self," said the mate, as he disappeared below. His head suddenly appeared again over the companion. "If some people don't," he added, and disappeared again.

He was pleased to notice as he ate his dinner that the giddy prattle above had ceased, and with his back turned toward the couple when he appeared on deck again, he lounged slowly forward until the skipper called him back again.

"Wot was them words you said just now, Ted?" he inquired.

The mate repeated them with gusto.

"Very good," said the skipper, sharply; "very good."

"Don't you ever speak to me again," said Miss Harris, with a stately air, "because I won't answer you if you do."

The mate displayed more of his schoolboy nature. "Wait till you're spoken to," he said, rudely. "This is your gratefulness, I suppose?"

"Gratefulness?" said Miss Harris, with her chin in the air. "What for?"

"For bringing you for a trip," replied the mate, sternly.

"You bringing me for a trip!" said Miss Harris, scornfully. "Captain Gibbs is the master here, I suppose. He is giving me the trip. You're only the mate."

"Just so," said the mate, with a grin at his brother-in-law, which made that worthy shift uneasily. "I wonder what Loo will say when she sees you with a lady aboard?"

"She came to please you," said Captain Gibbs, with haste.

"Ho! she did, did she?" jeered the mate. "Prove it; only don't look to me to back you, that's all."

The other eyed him in consternation, and his manner changed.

"Don't play the fool, Ted," he said, not unkindly; "you know what Loo is."

"Well, I'm reckoning on that," said the mate, deliberately. "I'm going for'ard; don't let me interrupt you two. So long."

He went slowly forward, and lighting his pipe, sprawled carelessly on the deck, and renounced the entire sex forthwith. At teatime the skipper attempted to reverse the procedure at the other meals; but as Miss Harris steadfastly declined to sit at the same table as the mate, his good intentions came to naught.

He made an appeal to what he termed the mate's better nature, after Miss Harris had retired to the seclusion of her bed-chamber, but in vain.

"She's nothing to do with me," declared the mate, majestically. "I wash my hands of her. She's a flirt. I'm like Louisa, I can't bear flirts."

The skipper said no more, but his face was so worn that Miss Harris, when she came on deck in the early morning and found the barge gliding gently between the grassy banks of a river, attributed it to the difficulty of navigating so large a craft on so small and winding a stream.

"We shall be alongside in 'arf an hour," said the skipper, eyeing her.

Miss Harris expressed her gratification.

"P'raps you wouldn't mind going down the fo'c'sle and staying there till we've made fast," said the other. "I'd take it as a favour. My owners don't like me to carry passengers."

Miss Harris, who understood perfectly, said, "Certainly," and with a cold stare at the mate, who was at no pains to conceal his amusement, went below at once, thoughtfully closing the scuttle after her.

"There's no call to make mischief, Ted," said the skipper, somewhat anxiously, as they swept round the last bend and came into view of Coalsham.

The mate said nothing, but stood by to take in sail as they ran swiftly toward the little quay. The pace slackened, and the Arabella, as though conscious of the contraband in her forecastle, crept slowly to where a stout, middle-aged woman, who bore a strong likeness to the mate, stood upon the quay.

"There's poor Loo," said the mate, with a sigh.

The skipper made no reply to this infernal insinuation. The barge ran alongside the quay and made fast.

"I thought you'd be up," said Mrs. Gibbs to her husband. "Now come along to breakfast; Ted 'll follow on."

Captain Gibbs, dived down below for his coat, and slipping ashore, thankfully prepared to move off with his wife.

"Come on as soon as you can, Ted," said the latter. "Why, what on earth is he making that face for?"

She turned in amazement as her brother, making a pretence of catching her husband's eye, screwed his face up into a note of interrogation and gave a slight jerk with his thumb.

"Come along," said Captain Gibbs, taking her arm with much affection.

"But what's Ted looking like that for?" demanded his wife, as she easily intercepted another choice facial expression of the mate's.

"Oh, it's his fun," replied her husband, walking on.

"Fun?" repeated Mrs. Gibbs, sharply. "What's the matter, Ted."

"Nothing," replied the mate.

"Touch o' toothache," said the skipper. "Come along, Loo; I can just do with one o' your breakfasts."

Mrs. Gibbs suffered herself to be led on, and had got at least five yards on the way home, when she turned and looked back. The mate had still got the toothache, and was at that moment in all the agonies of a phenomenal twinge.

"There's something wrong here," said Mrs. Gibbs as she retraced her steps. "Ted, what are you making that face for?"

"It's my own face," said the mate, evasively.

Mrs. Gibbs conceded the point, and added bitterly that it couldn't be helped. All the same she wanted to know what he meant by it.

"Ask John," said the vindictive mate.

Mrs. Gibbs asked. Her husband said he didn't know, and added that Ted had been like it before, but he had not told her for fear of frightening her. Then he tried to induce her to go with him to the chemist's to get something for it.

Mrs. Gibbs shook her head firmly, and boarding the barge, took a seat on the hatch and proceeded to catechise her brother as to his symptoms. He denied that there was anything the matter with him, while his eyes openly sought those of Captain Gibbs as though asking for instruction.

"You come home, Ted," she said at length.

"I can't," said the mate. "I can't leave the ship."

"Why not?" demanded his sister.

"Ask John," said the mate again.

At this Mrs. Gibbs's temper, which had been rising, gave way altogether, and she stamped fiercely upon the deck. A stamp of the foot has been for all time a rough-and-ready means of signalling; the fore-scuttle was drawn back, and the face of a young and pretty girl appeared framed in the opening. The mate raised his eyebrows with a helpless gesture, and as for the unfortunate skipper, any jury would have found him guilty without leaving the box. The wife of his bosom, with a flaming visage, turned and regarded him.

"You villain!" she said, in a choking voice.

Captain Gibbs caught his breath and looked appealingly at the mate.

"It's a little surprise for you, my dear," he faltered, "it's Ted's young lady."

"Nothing of the kind," said the mate, sharply.

"It's not? How dare you say such a thing?" demanded Miss Harris, stepping on to the deck.

"Well, you brought her aboard, Ted, you know you did," pleaded the unhappy skipper.

The mate did not deny it, but his face was so full of grief and surprise that the other's heart sank within him.

"All right," said the mate at last; "have it your own way."

"Hold your tongue, Ted," shouted Mrs. Gibbs; "you're trying to shield him."

"I tell you Ted brought her aboard, and they had a lover's quarrel," said her unhappy spouse. "It's nothing to do with me at all."

"And that's why you told me Ted had got the toothache, and tried to get me off to the chemist's, I s'pose," retorted his wife, with virulence. "Do you think I'm a fool? How dare you ask a young woman on this barge? How dare you?"

"I didn't ask her," said her husband.

"I s'pose she came without being asked," sneered his wife, turning her regards to the passenger; "she looks the sort that might. You brazen-faced girl!"

"Here, go easy, Loo," interrupted the mate, flushing as he saw the girl's pale face.

"Mind your own business," said his sister, violently.

"It is my business," said the repentant mate. "I brought her aboard, and then we quarrelled."

"I've no doubt," said his sister, bitterly; "it's very pretty, but it won't do."

"I swear it's the truth," said the mate.

"Why did John keep it so quiet and hide her for, then?" demanded his sister.

"I came down for the trip," said Miss Harris; "that is all about it. There is nothing to make a fuss about. How much is it, Captain Gibbs?"

She produced a little purse from her pocket, but before the embarrassed skipper could reply, his infuriated wife struck it out of her hand. The mate sprang instinctively forward, but too late, and the purse fell with a splash into the water. The girl gave a faint cry and clasped her hands.

"How am I to get back?" she gasped.

"I'll see to that, Lucy," said the mate. "I'm very sorry—I've been a brute."

"You?" said the indignant girl. "I would sooner drown myself than be beholden to you."

"I'm very sorry," repeated the mate, humbly.

"There s enough of this play-acting," interposed Mrs. Gibbs. "Get off this barge."

"You stay where you are," said the mate, authoritatively.

"Send that girl off this barge," screamed Mrs. Gibbs to her husband.

Captain Gibbs smiled in a silly fashion and scratched his head. "Where is she to go?" he asked feebly.

"Wh'at does it matter to you where she goes?" cried his wife, fiercely. "Send her off."

The girl eyed her haughtily, and repulsing the mate as he strove to detain her, stepped to the side. Then she paused as he suddenly threw off his coat, and sitting down on the hatch, hastily removed his boots. The skipper, divining his intentions, seized him by the arm.

"Don't be a fool, Ted," he gasped; "you'll get under the barge."

The mate shook him off, and went in with a splash which half drowned his adviser. Miss Harris, clasping her hands, ran to the side and gazed fearfully at the spot where he had disappeared, while his sister in a terrible voice seized the opportunity to point out to her husband the probably fatal results of his ill-doing. There was an anxious interval, and then the mate's head appeared above the water, and after a breathing-space disappeared again. The skipper, watching uneasily, stood by with a lifebelt.

"Come out, Ted," screamed his sister as he came up for breath again.

The mate disappeared once more, but coming up for the third time, hung on to the side of the barge to recover a bit. A clothed man in the water savours of disaster and looks alarming. Miss Harris began to cry.

"You'll be drowned," she whimpered.

"Come out," said Mrs. Gibbs, in a raspy voice. She knelt on the deck and twined her fingers in his hair. The mate addressed her in terms rendered brotherly by pain.

"Never mind about the purse," sobbed Miss Harris; "it doesn't matter."

"Will you make it up if I come out, then," demanded the diver.

"No; I'll never speak to you again as long as I live," said the girl, passionately.

The mate disappeared again. This time he was out of sight longer than usual, and when he came up merely tossed his arms weakly and went down again. There was a scream from the women, and a mighty splash as the skipper went overboard with a life-belt. The mate's head, black and shining, showed for a moment; the skipper grabbed him by the hair and towed him to the barge's side, and in the midst of a considerable hubbub both men were drawn from the water.

The skipper shook himself like a dog, but the mate lay on the deck inert in a puddle of water. Mrs. Gibbs frantically slapped his hands; and Miss Harris, bending over him, rendered first aid by kissing him wildly.

Captain Gibbs pushed her away. "He won't come round while you're a-kissing of him," he cried, roughly.

To his indignant surprise the drowned man opened one eye and winked acquiescence. The skipper dropped his arms by his side and stared at him stupidly.

"I saw his eyelid twitch," cried Mrs. Gibbs, joyfully.

"He's all right," said her indignant husband; "'e ain't born to be drowned, 'e ain't. I've spoilt a good suit of clothes for nothing."

To his wife's amazement, he actually walked away from the insensible man, and with a boathook reached for his hat, which was floating by. Mrs. Gibbs, still gazing in blank astonishment, caught a seraphic smile on the face of her brother as Miss Harris continued her ministrations, and in a pardonable fit of temper the overwrought woman gave him a box on the ear, which brought him round at once.

"Where am I?" he inquired, artlessly.

Mrs. Gibbs told him. She also told him her opinion of him, and without plagiarizing her husband's words, came to the same conclusion as to his ultimate fate.

"You come along home with me," she said, turning in a friendly fashion to the bewildered girl. "They deserve what they've got—both of 'em. I only hope that they'll both get such awful colds that they won't find their voices for a twelvemonth."

She took the girl by the arm and helped her ashore. They turned their heads once in the direction of the barge, and saw the justly incensed skipper keeping the mate's explanations and apologies at bay with a boat-hook. Then they went in to breakfast.

LAWYER QUINCE

Lawyer Quince, so called by his neighbours in Little Haven from his readiness at all times to place at their disposal the legal lore he had acquired from a few old books while following his useful occupation of making boots, sat in a kind of wooden hutch at the side of his cottage plying his trade. The London coach had gone by in a cloud of dust some three hours before, and since then the wide village street had slumbered almost undisturbed in the sunshine.

Hearing footsteps and the sound of voices raised in dispute caused him to look up from his work. Mr. Rose, of Holly Farm, Hogg, the miller, and one or two neighbours of lesser degree appeared to be in earnest debate over some point of unusual difficulty.

Lawyer Quince took a pinch of snuff and bent to his work again. Mr. Rose was one of the very few who openly questioned his legal knowledge, and his gibes concerning it were only too frequent. Moreover, he had a taste for practical joking, which to a grave man was sometimes offensive.

"Well, here he be," said Mr. Hogg to the farmer, as the group halted in front of the hutch. "Now ask Lawyer Quince and see whether I ain't told you true. I'm willing to abide by what he says."

Mr. Quince put down his hammer and, brushing a little snuff from his coat, leaned back in his chair and eyed them with grave confidence.

"It's like this," said the farmer. "Young Pascoe has been hanging round after my girl Celia, though I told her she wasn't to have nothing to do with him. Half an hour ago I was going to put my pony in its stable when I see a young man sitting there waiting."

"Well?" said Mr. Quince, after a pause.

"He's there yet," said the farmer. "I locked him in, and Hogg here says that I've got the right to keep him locked up there as long as I like. I say it's agin the law, but Hogg he says no. I say his folks would come and try to break open my stable, but Hogg says if they do I can have the law of 'em for damaging my property."

"So you can," interposed Mr. Hogg, firmly. "You see whether Lawyer Quince don't say I'm right."

Mr. Quince frowned, and in order to think more deeply closed his eyes. Taking advantage of this three of his auditors, with remarkable unanimity, each closed one.

"It's your stable," said Mr. Quince, opening his eyes and speaking with great deliberation, "and you have a right to lock it up when you like."

"There you are," said Mr. Hogg; "what did I tell you?"

"If anybody's there that's got no business there, that's his look-out," continued Mr. Quince. "You didn't induce him to go in?"

"Certainly not," replied the farmer.

"I told him he can keep him there as long as he likes," said the jubilant Mr. Hogg, "and pass him in bread and water through the winder; it's got bars to it."

"Yes," said Mr. Quince, nodding, "he can do that. As for his folks knocking the place about, if you like to tie up one or two of them nasty, savage dogs of yours to the stable, well, it's your stable, and you can fasten your dogs to it if you like. And you've generally got a man about the yard."

Mr. Hogg smacked his thigh in ecstasy.

"But—" began the farmer.

"That's the law," said the autocratic Mr. Quince, sharply. "O' course, if you think you know more about it than I do, I've nothing more to say."

"I don't want to do nothing I could get into trouble for," murmured Mr. Rose.

"You can't get into trouble by doing as I tell you," said the shoemaker, impatiently. "However, to be quite on the safe side, if I was in your place I should lose the key."

"Lose the key?" said the farmer, blankly.

"Lose the key," repeated the shoemaker, his eyes watering with intense appreciation of his own resourcefulness. "You can find it any time you want to, you know. Keep him there till he promises to give up your daughter, and tell him that as soon as he does you'll have a hunt for the key."

Mr. Rose regarded him with what the shoemaker easily understood to be speechless admiration.

"I—I'm glad I came to you," said the farmer, at last.

"You're welcome," said the shoemaker, loftily. "I'm always ready to give advice to them as require it."

"And good advice it is," said the smiling Mr. Hogg. "Why don't you behave yourself, Joe Garnham?" he demanded, turning fiercely on a listener.

Mr. Garnham, whose eyes were watering with emotion, attempted to explain, but, becoming hysterical, thrust a huge red handkerchief to his mouth and was led away by a friend. Mr. Quince regarded his departure with mild disdain.

"Little things please little minds," he remarked.

"So they do," said Mr. Hogg. "I never thought—What's the matter with you, George Askew?"

Mr. Askew, turning his back on him, threw up his hands with a helpless gesture and followed in the wake of Mr. Garnham. Mr. Hogg appeared to be about to apologise, and then suddenly altering his mind made a hasty and unceremonious exit, accompanied by the farmer.

Mr. Quince raised his eyebrows and then, after a long and meditative pinch of snuff, resumed his work. The sun went down and the light faded slowly; distant voices sounded close on the still evening air, snatches of hoarse laughter jarred upon his ears. It was clear that the story of the imprisoned swain was giving pleasure to Little Haven.

He rose at last from his chair and, stretching his long, gaunt frame, removed his leather apron, and after a wash at the pump went into the house. Supper was laid, and he gazed with approval on the home-made sausage rolls, the piece of cold pork, and the cheese which awaited his onslaught.

"We won't wait for Ned," said Mrs. Quince, as she brought in a jug of ale and placed it by her husband's elbow.

Mr. Quince nodded and filled his glass.

"You've been giving more advice, I hear," said Mrs. Quince.

Her husband, who was very busy, nodded again.

"It wouldn't make no difference to young Pascoe's chance, anyway," said Mrs. Quince, thoughtfully.

Mr. Quince continued his labours. "Why?" he inquired, at last.

His wife smiled and tossed her head.

"Young Pascoe's no chance against our Ned," she said, swelling with maternal pride.

"Eh?" said the shoemaker, laying down his knife and fork. "Our Ned?"

"They are as fond of each other as they can be," said Mrs. Quince, "though I don't suppose Farmer Rose'll care for it; not but what our Ned's as good as he is."

"Is Ned up there now?" demanded the shoemaker, turning pale, as the mirthful face of Mr. Garnham sudden y occurred to him.

"Sure to be," tittered his wife. "And to think o' poor young Pascoe shut up in that stable while he's courting Celia!"

Mr. Quince took up his knife and fork again, but his appetite had gone. Whoever might be paying attention to Miss Rose at that moment he felt quite certain that it was not Mr. Ned Quince, and he trembled with anger as he saw the absurd situation into which the humorous Mr. Rose had led him. For years Little Haven had accepted his decisions as final and boasted of his sharpness to neighbouring hamlets, and many a cottager had brought his boots to be mended a whole week before their time for the sake of an interview.

He moved his chair from the table and smoked a pipe. Then he rose, and putting a couple of formidable law-books under his arm, walked slowly down the road in the direction of Holly Farm.

The road was very quiet and the White Swan, usually full at this hour, was almost deserted, but if any doubts as to the identity of the prisoner lingered in his mind they were speedily dissipated by the behaviour of the few customers who crowded to the door to see him pass.

A hum of voices fell on his ear as he approached the farm; half the male and a goodly proportion of the female population of Little Haven were leaning against the fence or standing in little knots in the road, while a few of higher social status stood in the farm-yard itself.

"Come down to have a look at the prisoner?" inquired the farmer, who was standing surrounded by a little group of admirers.

"I came down to see you about that advice I gave you this afternoon," said Mr. Quince.

"Ah!" said the other.

"I was busy when you came," continued Mr. Quince, in a voice of easy unconcern, "and I gave you advice from memory. Looking up the subject after you'd gone I found that I was wrong."

"You don't say so?" said the farmer, uneasily. "If I've done wrong I'm only doing what you told me I could do."

"Mistakes will happen with the best of us," said the shoemaker, loudly, for the benefit of one or two murmurers. "I've known a man to marry a woman for her money before now and find out afterward that she hadn't got any."

One unit of the group detached itself and wandered listlessly toward the gate.

"Well, I hope I ain't done nothing wrong," said Mr. Rose, anxiously. "You gave me the advice; there's men here as can prove it. I don't want to do nothing agin the law. What had I better do?"

"Well, if I was you," said Mr. Quince, concealing his satisfaction with difficulty, "I should let him out at once and beg his pardon, and say you hope he'll do nothing about it. I'll put in a word for you if you like with old Pascoe."

Mr. Rose coughed and eyed him queerly.

"You're a Briton," he said, warmly. "I'll go and let him out at once."

He strode off to the stable, despite the protests of Mr. Hogg, and, standing by the door, appeared to be deep in thought; then he came back slowly, feeling in his pockets as he walked.

"William," he said, turning toward Mr. Hogg, "I s'pose you didn't happen to notice where I put that key?"

"That I didn't," said Mr. Hogg, his face clearing suddenly.

"I had it in my hand not half an hour ago," said the agitated Mr. Rose, thrusting one hand into his trouser-pocket and groping. "It can't be far."

Mr. Quince attempted to speak, and, failing, blew his nose violently.

"My memory ain't what it used to be," said the farmer. "Howsomever, I dare say it'll turn up in a day or two."

"You—you'd better force the door," suggested Mr. Quince, struggling to preserve an air of judicial calm.

"No, no," said Mr. Rose; "I ain't going to damage my property like that. I can lock my stable-door and unlock it when I like; if people get in there as have no business there, it's their look-out."

"That's law," said Mr. Hogg; "I'll eat my hat if it ain't."

"Do you mean to tell me you've really lost the key?" demanded Mr. Quince, eyeing the farmer sternly.

"Seems like it," said Mr. Rose. "However, he won't come to no hurt. I'll put in some bread and water for him, same as you advised me to."

Mr. Quince mastered his wrath by an effort, and with no sign of discomposure moved away without making any reference to the identity of the unfortunate in the stable."

"Good-night," said the farmer, "and thank you for coming and giving me the fresh advice. It ain't everybody that 'ud ha' taken the trouble. If I hadn't lost that key—"

The shoemaker scowled, and with the two fat books under his arm passed the listening neighbours with the air of a thoughtful man out for an evening stroll. Once inside his house, however, his manner changed, the attitude of Mrs. Quince demanding, at any rate, a show of concern.

"It's no good talking," he said at last. "Ned shouldn't have gone there, and as for going to law about it, I sha'n't do any such thing; I should never hear the end of it. I shall just go on as usual, as if nothing had happened, and when Rose is tired of keeping him there he must let him out. I'll bide my time."

Mrs. Quince subsided into vague mutterings as to what she would do if she were a man, coupled with sundry aspersions upon the character, looks, and family connections of Farmer Rose, which somewhat consoled her for being what she was.

"He has always made jokes about your advice," she said at length, "and now everybody'll think he's right. I sha'n't be able to look anybody in the face. I should have seen through it at once if it had been me. I'm going down to give him a bit o' my mind."

"You stay where you are," said Mr. Quince, sharply, "and, mind, you are not to talk about it to anybody. Farmer Rose 'ud like nothing better than to see us upset about it. I ain't done with him yet. You wait."

Mrs. Quince, having no option, waited, but nothing happened. The following day found Ned Quince still a prisoner, and, considering the circumstances, remarkably cheerful. He declined point-blank to renounce his preposterous attentions, and said that, living on the premises, he felt half like a son-in-law already. He also complimented the farmer upon the quality of his bread.

The next morning found him still unsubdued, and, under interrogation from the farmer, he admitted that he liked it, and said that the feeling of being at home was growing upon him.

"If you're satisfied, I am," said Mr. Rose, grimly. "I'll keep you here till you promise; mind that."

"It's a nobleman's life," said Ned, peeping through the window, "and I'm beginning to like you as much as my real father."

"I don't want none o' yer impudence," said the farmer, reddening.

"You'll like me better when you've had me here a little longer," said Ned; "I shall grow on you. Why not be reasonable and make up your mind to it? Celia and I have."

"I'm going to send Celia away on Saturday," said Mr. Rose; "make yourself happy and comfortable in here till then. If you'd like another crust o' bread or an extra half pint o' water you've only got to mention it. When she's gone I'll have a hunt for that key, so as you can go back to your father and help him to understand his law-books better."

He strode off with the air of a conqueror, and having occasion to go to the village looked in at the shoe-maker's window as he passed and smiled broadly. For years Little Haven had regarded Mr. Quince with awe, as being far too dangerous a man for the lay mind to tamper with, and at one stroke the farmer had revealed the hollowness of his pretensions. Only that morning the wife of a labourer had called and asked him to hurry the mending of a pair of boots. She was a voluble woman, and having overcome her preliminary nervousness more than hinted that if he gave less time to the law and more to his trade it would be better for himself and everybody else.

Miss Rose accepted her lot in a spirit of dutiful resignation, and on Saturday morning after her father's admonition not to forget that the coach left the White Swan at two sharp, set off to pay a few farewell visits. By half-past twelve she had finished, and Lawyer Quince becoming conscious of a shadow on his work looked up to see her standing before the window. He replied to a bewitching smile with a short nod and became intent upon his work again.

For a short time Celia lingered, then to his astonishment she opened the gate and walked past the side of the house into the garden. With growing astonishment he observed her enter his tool-shed and close the door behind her.

For ten minutes he worked on and then, curiosity getting the better of him, he walked slowly to the tool-shed and, opening the door a little way, peeped in. It was a small shed, crowded with agricultural implements. The floor was occupied by an upturned wheelbarrow, and sitting on the barrow, with her soft cheek leaning against the wall, sat Miss Rose fast asleep. Mr. Quince coughed several times, each cough being louder than the last, and then, treading softly, was about to return to the workshop when the girl stirred and muttered in her sleep. At first she was unintelligible, then he distinctly caught the words "idiot" and "blockhead."

"She's dreaming of somebody," said Mr. Quince to himself with conviction.

"Wonder who it is?"

"Can't see—a thing—under—his—nose," murmured the fair sleeper.

"Celia!" said Mr. Quince, sharply. "Celia!"

He took a hoe from the wall and prodded her gently with the handle. A singularly vicious expression marred the soft features, but that was all.

"Ce-lia!" said the shoemaker, who feared sun-stroke.

"Fancy if he—had—a moment's common sense," murmured Celia, drowsily, "and locked—the door."

Lawyer Quince dropped the hoe with a clatter and stood regarding her open-mouthed. He was a careful man with his property, and the stout door boasted a good lock. He sped to the house on tip-toe, and taking the key from its nail on the kitchen dresser returned to the shed, and after another puzzled glance at the sleeping girl locked her in.

For half an hour he sat in silent enjoyment of the situation—enjoyment which would have been increased if he could have seen Mr. Rose standing at the gate of Holly Farm, casting anxious glances up and down the road. Celia's luggage had gone down to the White Swan, and an excellent cold luncheon was awaiting her attention in the living-room.

Half-past one came and no Celia, and five minutes later two farm labourers and a boy lumbered off in different directions in search of the missing girl, with instructions that she was to go straight to the White Swan to meet the coach. The farmer himself walked down to the inn, turning over in his mind a heated lecture composed for the occasion, but the coach came and, after a cheerful bustle and the consumption of sundry mugs of beer, sped on its way again.

He returned home in silent consternation, seeking in vain for a satisfactory explanation of the mystery. For a robust young woman to disappear in broad day-light and leave no trace behind her was extraordinary. Then a sudden sinking sensation in the region of the waistcoat and an idea occurred simultaneously.

He walked down to the village again, the idea growing steadily all the way. Lawyer Quince was hard at work, as usual, as he passed. He went by the window three times and gazed wistfully at the cottage. Coming to the conclusion at last that two heads were better than one in such a business, he walked on to the mill and sought Mr. Hogg.

"That's what it is," said the miller, as he breathed his suspicions. "I thought all along Lawyer Quince would have the laugh of you. He's wonderful deep. Now, let's go to work cautious like. Try and look as if nothing had happened."

Mr. Rose tried.

"Try agin," said the miller, with some severity. "Get the red out o' your face and let your eyes go back and don't look as though you're going to bite somebody."

Mr. Rose swallowed an angry retort, and with an attempt at careless ease sauntered up the road with the miller to the shoemaker's. Lawyer Quince was still busy, and looked up inquiringly as they passed before him.

"I s'pose," said the diplomatic Mr. Hogg, who was well acquainted with his neighbour's tidy and methodical habits—"I s'pose you couldn't lend me your barrow for half an hour? The wheel's off mine."

Mr. Quince hesitated, and then favoured him with a glance intended to remind him of his scurvy behaviour three days before.

"You can have it," he said at last, rising.

Mr. Hogg pinched his friend in his excitement, and both watched Mr. Quince with bated breath as he took long, slow strides toward the tool-shed. He tried the door and then went into the house, and even before his reappearance both gentlemen knew only too well what was about to happen. Red was all too poor a word to apply to Mr. Rose's countenance as the shoemaker came toward them, feeling in his waist-coat pocket with hooked fingers and thumb, while Mr. Hogg's expressive features were twisted into an appearance of rosy appreciation.

"Did you want the barrow very particular?" inquired the shoemaker, in a regretful voice.

"Very particular," said Mr. Hogg.

Mr. Quince went through the performance of feeling in all his pockets, and then stood meditatively rubbing his chin.

"The door's locked," he said, slowly, "and what I've done with that there key—"

"You open that door," vociferated Mr. Rose, "else I'll break it in. You've got my daughter in that shed and I'm going to have her out."

"Your daughter?" said Mr. Quince, with an air of faint surprise. "What should she be doing in my shed?"

"You let her out," stormed Mr. Rose, trying to push past him.

"Don't trespass on my premises," said Lawyer Quince, interposing his long, gaunt frame. "If you want that door opened you'll have to wait till my boy Ned comes home. I expect he knows where to find the key."

Mr. Rose's hands fell limply by his side and his tongue, turning prudish, refused its office. He turned and stared at Mr. Hogg in silent consternation.

"Never known him to be beaten yet," said that admiring weather-cock.

"Ned's been away three days," said the shoemaker, "but I expect him home soon."

Mr. Rose made a strange noise in his throat and then, accepting his defeat, set off at a rapid pace in the direction of home. In a marvellously short space of time, considering his age and figure, he was seen returning with Ned Quince, flushed and dishevelled, walking by his side.

"Here he is," said the farmer. "Now where's that key?"

Lawyer Quince took his son by the arm and led him into the house, from whence they almost immediately emerged with Ned waving the key.

"I thought it wasn't far," said the sapient Mr. Hogg.

Ned put the key in the lock and flinging the door open revealed Celia Rose, blinking and confused in the sudden sunshine. She drew back as she saw her father and began to cry with considerable fervour.

"How did you get in that shed, miss?" demanded her parent, stamping.

Miss Rose trembled.

"I—I went there," she sobbed. "I didn't want to go away."

"Well, you'd better stay there," shouted the over-wrought Mr. Rose. "I've done with you. A girl that 'ud turn against her own father I—I—"

He drove his right fist into his left palm and stamped out into the road. Lawyer Quince and Mr. Hogg, after a moment's hesitation, followed.

"The laugh's agin you, farmer," said the latter gentleman, taking his arm.

Mr. Rose shook him off.

"Better make the best of it," continued the peace-maker.

"She's a girl to be proud of," said Lawyer Quince, keeping pace with the farmer on the other side. "She's got a head that's worth yours and mine put together, with Hogg's thrown in as a little makeweight."

"And here's the White Swan," said Mr. Hogg, who had a hazy idea of a compliment, "and all of us as dry as a bone. Why not all go in and have a glass to shut folks' mouths?"

"And cry quits," said the shoemaker.

"And let bygones be bygones," said Mr. Hogg, taking the farmer's arm again.

Mr. Rose stopped and shook his head obstinately, and then, under the skilful pilotage of Mr. Hogg, was steered in the direction of the hospitable doors of the White Swan. He made a last bid for liberty on the step and then disappeared inside. Lawyer Quince brought up the rear.

On a fine spring morning in the early part of the present century, Tetby, a small port on the east coast, was keeping high holiday. Tradesmen left their shops, and labourers their work, and flocked down to join the maritime element collected on the quay.

In the usual way Tetby was a quiet, dull little place, clustering in a tiny heap of town on one side of the river, and perching in scattered red-tiled cottages on the cliffs of the other.

Now, however, people were grouped upon the stone quay, with its litter of fish-baskets and coils of rope, waiting expectantly, for to-day the largest ship ever built in Tetby, by Tetby hands, was to start upon her first voyage.

As they waited, discussing past Tetby ships, their builders, their voyages, and their fate, a small piece of white sail showed on the noble barque from her moorings up the river. The groups on the quay grew animated as more sail was set, and in a slow and stately fashion the new ship drew near. As the light breeze took her sails she came faster, sitting the water like a duck, her lofty masts tapering away to the sky as they broke through the white clouds of canvas. She passed within ten fathoms of the quay, and the men cheered and the women held their children up to wave farewell, for she was manned from captain to cabin boy by Tetby men, and bound for the distant southern seas.

Outside the harbour she altered her course somewhat and bent, like a thing of life, to the wind blowing outside. The crew sprang into the rigging and waved their caps, and kissed their grimy hands to receding Tetby. They were answered by rousing cheers from the shore, hoarse and masculine, to drown the lachrymose attempts of the women.

They watched her until their eyes were dim, and she was a mere white triangular speck on the horizon. Then, like a melting snowflake, she vanished into air, and the Tetby folk, some envying the bold mariners, and others thankful that their lives were cast upon the safe and pleasant shore, slowly dispersed to their homes.

Months passed, and the quiet routine of Tetby went on undisturbed. Other craft came into port and, discharging and loading in an easy, comfortable fashion, sailed again. The keel of another ship was being laid in the shipyard, and slowly the time came round when the return of Tetby's Pride, for so she was named, might be reasonably looked for.

It was feared that she might arrive in the night—the cold and cheerless night, when wife and child were abed, and even if roused to go down on to the quay would see no more of her than her side-lights staining the water, and her dark form stealing cautiously up the river. They would have her come by day. To see her first on that horizon, into which she had dipped and vanished. To see her come closer and closer, the good stout ship seasoned by southern seas and southern suns, with the crew crowding the sides to gaze at Tetby, and see how the children had grown.

But she came not. Day after day the watchers waited for her in vain. It was whispered at length that she was overdue, and later on, but only by those who had neither kith nor kin aboard of her, that she was missing.

Long after all hope had gone wives and mothers, after the manner of their kind, watched and waited on the cheerless quay. One by one they stayed away, and forgot the dead to attend to the living.

Babes grew into sturdy, ruddy-faced boys and girls, boys and girls into young men and women, but no news of the missing ship, no word from the missing men. Slowly year succeeded year, and the lost ship became a legend. The man who had built her was old and grey, and time had smoothed away the sorrows of the bereaved.

It was on a dark, blustering September night that an old woman sat by her fire knitting. The fire was low, for it was more for the sake of company than warmth, and it formed an agreeable contrast to the wind which whistled round the house, bearing on its wings the sound of the waves as they came crashing ashore.

"God help those at sea to-night," said the old woman devoutly, as a stronger gust than usual shook the house.

She put her knitting in her lap and clasped her hands, and at that moment the cottage door opened. The lamp flared and smoked up the chimney with the draught, and then went out. As the old woman rose from her seat the door closed.

"Who's there?" she cried nervously.

Her eyes were dim and the darkness sudden, but she fancied she saw something standing by the door, and snatching a spill from the mantelpiece she thrust it into the fire, and relit the lamp.

A man stood on the threshold, a man of middle age, with white drawn face and scrubby beard. His clothes were in rags, his hair unkempt, and his light grey eyes sunken and tired.

The old woman looked at him, and waited for him to speak. When he did so he took a step towards her, and said—

"Mother!"

With a great cry she threw herself upon his neck and strained him to her withered bosom, and kissed him. She could not believe her eyes, her senses, but clasped him convulsively, and bade him speak again, and wept, and thanked God, and laughed all in a breath.

Then she remembered herself, and led him tottering to the old Windsor chair, thrust him in it, and quivering with excitement took food and drink from the cupboard and placed them before him. He ate hungrily, the old woman watching him, and standing by his side to keep his glass filled with the home-brewed beer. At times he would have spoken, but she motioned him to silence and bade him eat, the tears coursing down her aged cheeks as she looked at his white famished face.

At length he laid down his knife and fork, and drinking off the ale, intimated that he had finished.

"My boy, my boy," said the old woman in a broken voice, "I thought you had gone down with Tetby's Pride long years ago."

He shook his head heavily.

"The captain and crew, and the good ship," asked his mother. "Where are they?"

"Captain—and—crew," said the son, in a strange hesitating fashion; "it is a long story—the ale has made me heavy. They are—"

He left off abruptly and closed his eyes.

"Where are they?" asked his mother. "What happened?"

He opened his eyes slowly.

"I—am—tired—dead tired. I have not—slept. I'll tell—you—morning."

He nodded again, and the old woman shook him gently.

"Go to bed then. Your old bed, Jem. It's as you left it, and it's made and the sheets aired. It's been ready for you ever since."

He rose to his feet, and stood swaying to and fro. His mother opened a door in the wall, and taking the lamp lighted him up the steep wooden staircase to the room he knew so well. Then he took her in his arms in a feeble hug, and kissing her on the forehead sat down wearily on the bed.

The old woman returned to her kitchen, and falling upon her knees remained for some time in a state of grateful, pious ecstasy. When she arose she thought of those other women, and, snatching a shawl from its peg behind the door, ran up the deserted street with her tidings.

In a very short time the town was astir. Like a breath of hope the whisper flew from house to house. Doors closed for the night were thrown open, and wondering children questioned their weeping mothers. Blurred images of husbands and fathers long since given over for dead stood out clear and distinct, smiling with bright faces upon their dear ones.

At the cottage door two or three people had already collected, and others were coming up the street in an unwonted bustle.

They found their way barred by an old woman,—a resolute old woman, her face still working with the great joy which had come into her old life, but who refused them admittance until her son had slept. Their thirst for news was uncontrollable, but with a swelling in her throat she realised that her share in Tetby's Pride was safe.

Women who had waited, and got patient at last after years of waiting, could not endure these additional few hours. Despair was endurable, but suspense! "Ah, God! Was their man alive? What did he look like? Had he aged much?"

"He was so fatigued he could scarce speak," said she. She had questioned him, but he was unable to reply. Give him but till the dawn, and they should know all.

So they waited, for to go home and sleep was impossible. Occasionally they moved a little way up the street, but never very far, and gathering in small knots excitedly discussed the great event It came to be understood that the rest of the crew had been cast away on an uninhabited island, it could be nothing else, and would doubtlessly soon be with them; all except one or two perhaps, who were old men when the ship sailed, and had probably died in the meantime. One said this in the hearing of an old woman whose husband, if alive, would be in extreme old age, but she smiled peacefully, albeit her lip trembled, and said she only expected to hear of him, that was all.

The suspense became almost unendurable. "Would this man never awake? Would it never be dawn?" The children were chilled with the wind, but their elders would scarcely have felt an Arctic frost With growing impatience they waited, glancing at times at two women who held themselves somewhat aloof from the others; two women who had married again, and whose second husbands waited, awkwardly enough, with them.

Slowly the weary windy night wore away, the old woman, deaf to their appeals, still keeping her door fast. The dawn was not yet, though the oft-consulted watches announced it near at hand. It was very close now, and the watchers collected by the door. It was undeniable that things were seen a little more distinctly. One could see better the grey, eager faces of his neighbours.

They knocked upon the door, and the old woman's eyes filled as she opened it and saw those faces. Unasked and unchid they invaded the cottage and crowded round the door.

"I will go up and fetch him," said the old woman.

If each could have heard the beating of the others' hearts, the noise would have been deafening, but as it was there was complete silence, except for some overwrought woman's sob.

The old woman opened the door leading to the room above, and with the slow, deliberate steps of age ascended the stairs, and those below heard her calling softly to her son.

Two or three minutes passed and she was heard descending the stairs again—alone. The smile, the pity, had left her face, and she seemed dazed and strange.

"I cannot wake him," she said piteously. "He sleeps so sound. He is fatigued. I have shaken him, but he still sleeps."

As she stopped, and looked appealingly round, the other old woman took her hand, and pressing it led her to a chair. Two of the men sprang quickly up the stairs. They were absent but a short while, and then they came down like men bewildered and distraught. No need to speak. A low wail of utter misery rose from the women, and was caught up and repeated by the crowd outside, for the only man who could have set their hearts at rest had escaped the perils of the deep, and died quietly in his bed.

LOW WATER

It was a calm, clear evening in late summer as the Elizabeth Ann, of Pembray, scorning the expensive aid of a tug, threaded her way down the London river under canvas. The crew were busy forward, and the master and part-owner—a fussy little man, deeply imbued with a sense of his own importance and cleverness—was at the wheel chatting with the mate. While waiting for a portion of his cargo, he had passed the previous week pleasantly enough with some relatives in Exeter, and was now in a masterful fashion receiving a report from the mate.

"There's one other thing," said the mate. "I dessay you've noticed how sober old Dick is to-night."

"I kept him short o' purpose," said the skipper, with a satisfied air.

"Tain't that," said the mate. "You'll be pleased to hear that 'im an' Sam has been talked over by the other two, and that all your crew now, 'cept the cook, who's still Roman Catholic, has j'ined the Salvation Army."

"Salvation Army!" repeated the skipper in dazed tones. "I don't want none o' your gammon, Bob."

"It's quite right," said the other. "You can take it from me. How it was done I don't know, but what I do know is, none of 'em has touched licker for five days. They've all got red jerseys, an' I hear as old Dick preaches a hexcellent sermon. He's red-hot on it, and t'others follow 'im like sheep."

"The drink's got to his brain," said the skipper sagely, after due reflection. "Well, I don't mind, so long as they behave theirselves."

He kept silence until Woolwich was passed, and they were running along with all sails set, and then, his curiosity being somewhat excited, he called old Dick to him, with the amiable intention of a little banter.

"What's this I hear about you j'ining the Salvation Army?" he asked.

"It's quite true, sir," said Dick. "I feel so happy, you can't think—we all do."

"Glory!" said one of the other men, with enthusiastic corroboration.

"Seems like the measles," said the skipper facetiously. "Four of you down with it at one time!"

"It IS like the measles, sir," said the old man impressively, "an' I only hope as you'll catch it yourself, bad."

"Hallelujah!" bawled the other man suddenly. "He'll catch it."

"Hold that noise, you, Joe!" shouted the skipper sternly. "How dare you make that noise aboard ship?"

"He's excited, sir," said Dick. "It's love for you in 'is 'eart as does it."

"Let him keep his love to hisself," said the skipper churlishly.

"Ah! that's just what we can't do," said Dick in high-pitched tones, which the skipper rightly concluded to be his preaching voice. "We can't do it—an' why can't we do it? Becos we feel good, an' we want you to feel good too. We want to share it with you. Oh, dear friend—"

"That's enough," said the master of the Elizabeth Ann, sharply. "Don't you go 'dear friending' me. Go for'ard! Go for'ard at once!"

With a melancholy shake of his head the old man complied, and the startled skipper turned to the mate, who was at the wheel, and expressed his firm intention of at once stopping such behaviour on his ship.

"You can't do it," said the mate firmly.

"Can't do it?" queried the skipper.

"Not a bit of it," said the other. "They've all got it bad, an' the more you get at 'em the wuss they'll be. Mark my words, best let 'em alone."

"I'll hold my hand a bit and watch 'em," was the reply; "but I've always been cap'n on my own ship, and I always will."

For the next twenty-four hours he retained his sovereignty undisputed, but on Sunday morning, after breakfast, when he was at the wheel, and the crew below, the mate, who had been forward, came aft with a strange grin struggling for development at the corners of his mouth.

"What's the matter?" inquired the skipper, regarding him with some disfavour.

"They're all down below with their red jerseys on," replied the mate, still struggling, "and they're holding a sort o' consultation about the lost lamb, an' the best way o' reaching 'is 'ard 'eart."

"Lost lamb!" repeated the skipper unconcernedly, but carefully avoiding the other's eye.

"You're the lost lamb," said the mate, who always went straight to the point.

"I won't have it," said the skipper excitably. "How dare they go on in this way? Go and send 'em up directly."

The mate, whistling cheerily, complied, and the four men, neatly attired in scarlet, came on deck.

"Now, what's all this nonsense about?" demanded the incensed man. "What do you want?"

"We want your pore sinful soul," said Dick with ecstasy.

"Ay, an' we'll have it," said Joe, with deep conviction.

"So we will," said the other two, closing their eyes and smiling rapturously; "so we will."

The skipper, alarmed, despite himself, at their confidence, turned a startled face to the mate.

"If you could see it now," continued Dick impressively, "you'd be frightened at it. If you could—"

"Get to your own end of the ship," spluttered the indignant skipper. "Get, before I kick you there!"

"Better let Sam have a try," said one of the other men, calmly ignoring the fury of the master; "his efforts have been wonderfully blessed. Come here, Sam."

"There's a time for everything" said Sam cautiously. "Let's go for'ard and do what we can for him among ourselves."

They moved off reluctantly, Dick throwing such affectionate glances at the skipper over his shoulders that he nearly choked with rage.

"I won't have it!" he said fiercely; "I'll knock it out of 'em."

"You can't," said the mate. "You can't knock sailor men about nowadays. The only thing you can do is to get rid of 'em."

"I don't want to do that," was the growling reply. "They've been with me a long time, and they're all good men. Why don't they have a go at you, I wonder?"

"ME?" said the mate, in indignant surprise. "Why, I'm a Seventh Day Baptist! They don't want to waste their time over me. I'm all right."

"You're a pretty Seventh Day Baptist, you are!" replied the skipper. "Fust I've heard of it."

"You don't understand about such things," said the mate.

"It must be a very easy religion," continued the skipper.

"I don't make a show of it, if that's what you mean," rejoined the other warmly. "I'm one o' them as believe in 'iding my light under a bushel."

"A pint pot'ud do easy," sneered the skipper. "It's more in your line, too."

"Anyway, the men reckernise it," said the mate loftily. "They don't go an' sit in their red jerseys an' hold mothers' meetings over me."

"I'll knock their blessed heads off!" growled the skipper. "I'll learn 'em to insult me!"

"It's all for your own good," said the other. "They mean it kindly. Well, I wish 'em luck."

With these hardy words he retired, leaving a seething volcano to pace the deck, and think over ways and means of once more reducing his crew to what he considered a fit and proper state of obedience and respect.

The climax was reached at tea-time, when an anonymous hand was thrust beneath the skylight, and a full-bodied tract fluttered wildly down and upset his tea.

"That's the last straw!" he roared, fishing out the tract and throwing it on the floor. "I'll read them chaps a lesson they won't forget in a hurry, and put a little money in my pocket at the same time. I've got a little plan in my 'ed as come to me quite sudden this afternoon. Come on deck, Bob."

Bob obeyed, grinning, and the skipper, taking the wheel from Sam, sent him for the others.

"Did you ever know me break my word, Dick?" he inquired abruptly, as they shuffled up.

"Never," said Dick.

"Cap'n Bowers' word is better than another man's oath," asseverated Joe.

"Well," said Captain Bowers, with a wink at the mate, "I'm going to give you chaps a little self-denial week all to yourselves. If you all live on biscuit and water till we get to port, and don't touch nothing else, I'll jine you and become a Salvationist."

"Biscuit and water," said Dick doubtfully, scratching a beard strong enough to scratch back.

"It wouldn't be right to play with our constitooshuns in that way, sir," objected Joe, shaking his head.

"There you are," said Bowers, turning to the mate with a wave of his hand. "They're precious anxious about me so long as it's confined to jawing, and dropping tracts into my tea, but when it comes to a little hardship on their part, see how they back out of it."

"We ain't backing out of it," said Dick cautiously; "but s'pose we do, how are we to be certain as you'll jine us?"

"You 've got my word for it," said the other, "an' the mate an' cook witness it."

"O' course, you jine the Army for good, sir," said Dick, still doubtfully.

"O' course."

"Then it's a bargain, sir," said Dick, beaming; "ain't it, chaps?"

"Ay, ay, ' said the others, but not beaming quite so much. "Oh, what a joyful day this is!" said the old man. "A Salvation crew an' a Salvation cap'n! We'll have the cook next, bad as he is."

"You'll have biskit an' water," said the cook icily, as they moved off, "an' nothing else, I'll take care."

"They must be uncommon fond o' me," said the skipper meditatively.

"Uncommon fond o' having their own way," growled the mate. "Nice thing you've let yourself in for."

"I know what I 'm about," was the confident reply.

"You ain't going to let them idiots fast for a week an' then break your word?" said the mate in surprise.

"Certainly not," said the other wrathfully; "I'd sooner jine three armies than do that, and you know it."

"They'll keep to the grub, don't you fear," said the mate. "I can't understand how you are going to manage it."

"That's where the brains come in," retorted the skipper, somewhat arrogantly.

"Fust time I've heard of 'em," murmured the mate softly; "but I s'pose you've been using pint pots too."

The skipper glared at him scornfully, but, being unprovided with a retort, forbore to reply, and going below again mixed himself a stiff glass of grog, and drank success to his scheme.

Three days passed, and the men stood firm, and, realising that they were slowly undermining the skipper's convictions, made no effort to carry him by direct assault. The mate made no attempt to conceal his opinion of his superior's peril, and in gloomy terms strove to put the full horror of his position before him.

"What your missis'll say the first time she sees you prancing up an' down the road tapping a tambourine, I can't think," said he.

"I shan't have no tambourine," said Captain Bowers cheerfully.

"It'll also be your painful dooty to stand outside your father-in-law's pub and try and persuade customers not to go in," continued Bob. "Nice thing that for a quiet family!"

The skipper smiled knowingly, and, rolling a cigar in his mouth, leaned back in his seat and cocked his eye at the skylight.

"Don't you worry, my lad," said he; "don't you worry. I'm in this job, an' I'm coming out on top. When men forget what's due to their betters, and preach to 'em, they've got to be taught what's what. If the wind keeps fair we ought to be home by Sunday night or Monday morning."

The other nodded.

"Now, you keep your eyes open," said the skipper; and, going to his state-room, he returned with three bottles of rum and a corkscrew, all of which, with an air of great mystery, he placed on the table, and then smiled at the mate. The mate smiled too.

"What's this?" inquired the skipper, drawing the cork, and holding a bottle under the other's nose.

"It smells like rum," said the mate, glancing round, possibly for a glass.

"It's for the men," said the skipper, "but you may take a drop."

The mate, taking down a glass, helped himself liberally, and, having made sure of it, sympathetically, but politely, expressed his firm opinion that the men would not touch it under any conditions whatever.

"You don't quite understand how firm they are," said he; you think it's just a new fad with 'em, but it ain't."

"They'll drink it," said the skipper, taking up two of the bottles. "Bring the other on deck for me."

The mate complied, wonderingly, and, laden with prime old Jamaica, ascended the steps.

"What's this?" inquired the skipper, crossing over to Dick, and holding out a bottle.

"Pison, sir," said Dick promptly.

"Have a drop," said the skipper jovially.

"Not for twenty pounds," said the old man, with a look of horror.

"Not for two million pounds," said Sam, with financial precision.

"Will anybody have a drop?" asked the owner, waving the bottle to and fro.

As he spoke a grimy paw shot out from behind him, and, before he quite realised the situation, the cook had accepted the invitation, and was hurriedly making the most of it.

"Not you," growled the skipper, snatching the bottle from him; "I didn't mean you. Well, my lads, if you won't have it neat you shall have it watered."

Before anybody could guess his intention he walked to the water-cask, and, removing the cover, poured in the rum. In the midst of a profound silence he emptied the three bottles, and then, with a triumphant smile, turned and confronted his astonished crew.

"What's in that cask, Dick?" he asked quietly.

"Rum and water," groaned Dick; "but that ain't fair play, sir. We've kep' to our part o' the agreement, sir, an' you ought to ha' kep' to yours."

"So I have," was the quick reply; "so I have, an' I still keep to it. Don't you see this, my lads; when you start playing antics with me you're playing a fool's game, an' you're bound to come a cropper. Some men would ha' waited longer afore they spiled their game, but I think you've suffered enough. Now there's a lump of beef and some taters on, an' you'd better go and make a good square meal, an' next time you want to alter the religion of people as knows better than you do, think twice."

"We don't want no beef, sir; biskit'll do for us," said Dick firmly.

"All right, please yourselves," said the skipper; "but mind, no hanky-panky, no coming for drink when my back's turned; this cask'll be watched; but if you do alter your mind about the beef you can tell the cook to get it for you any time you like."

He threw the bottles overboard, and, ignoring the groaning and head-shaking of the men, walked away, listening with avidity to the respectful tributes to his genius tendered by the mate and cook— flattery so delicate and so genuine withal that he opened another bottle.

"There's just one thing," said the mate presently; "won't the rum affect the cooking a good deal?"

"I never thought o' that," admitted the skipper; "still, we musn't expect to have everything our own way."

"No, no," said the mate blankly, admiring the other's choice of pronouns.

Up to Friday afternoon the skipper went about with a smile of kindly satisfaction on his face; but in the evening it weakened somewhat, and by Saturday morning it had vanished altogether, and was replaced by an expression of blank amazement and anxiety, for the crew shunned the water cask as though it were poison, without appearing to suffer the slightest inconvenience. A visible air of proprietorship appeared on their faces whenever they looked at the skipper, and the now frightened man inveighed fiercely to the mate against the improper methods of conversion patronised by some religious bodies, and the aggravating obstinacy of some of their followers.

"It's wonderful what enthusiasm'll do for a man," said Bob reflectively; "I knew a man once—"

"I don't want none o' your lies," interposed the other rudely.

"An' I don't want your blamed rum and water, if it comes to that," said the mate, firing up. "When a man's tea is made with rum, an' his beef is biled in it, he begins to wonder whether he's shipped with a seaman or a—a—"

"A what?" shouted the skipper. "Say it!"

"I can't think o' nothing foolish enough," was the frank reply. "It's all right for you, becos it's the last licker as you'll be allowed to taste, but it's rough on me and the cook."

"Damn you an' the cook," said the skipper, and went on deck to see whether the men's tongues were hanging out.

By Sunday morning he was frantic; the men were hale and well enough, though, perhaps, a trifle thin, and he began to believe with the cook that the age of miracles had not yet passed.

It was a broiling hot day, and, to add to his discomfort, the mate, who was consumed by a raging thirst, lay panting in the shade of the mainsail, exchanging condolences of a most offensive nature with the cook every time he looked his way.

All the morning he grumbled incessantly, until at length, warned by an offensive smell of rum that dinner was on the table, he got up and went below.

At the foot of the ladder he paused abruptly, for the skipper was leaning back in his seat, gazing in a fascinated manner at some object on the table.

"What's the matter?" inquired the mate in alarm.

The other, who did not appear to hear the question, made no answer, but continued to stare in a most extraordinary fashion at a bottle which graced the centre of the table.

"What is it?" inquired the mate, not venturing to trust his eyes. "WATER? Where did it come from?"

"Cook!" roared the skipper, turning a bloodshot eye on that worthy, as his pallid face showed behind the mate, "what's this? If you say it's water I'll kill you."

"I don't know what it is, sir," said the cook cautiously; "but Dick sent it to you with his best respects, and I was to say as there's plenty more where that came from. He's a nasty, under'anded, deceitful old man, is Dick, sir, an' it seems he laid in a stock o' water in bottles an' the like afore you doctored the cask, an' the men have had it locked up in their chests ever since."

"Dick's a very clever old man," remarked the mate, pouring himself out a glass, and drinking it with infinite relish, "ain't he, cap'n? It'll be a privilege to jine anything that man's connected with, won't it?"

He paused for a reply, but none came, for the cap'n, with dim eyes, was staring blankly into a future so lonely and uncongenial that he had lost the power of speech—even of that which, at other crises, had never failed to afford him relief. The mate gazed at him curiously for a moment, and then, imitating the example of the cook, quitted the cabin.

MADE TO MEASURE

Mr. Mott brought his niece home from the station with considerable pride. Although he had received a photograph to assist identification, he had been very dubious about accosting the pretty, well-dressed girl who had stepped from the train and gazed around with dove-like eyes in search of him. Now he was comfortably conscious of the admiring gaze of his younger fellow-townsmen.

"You'll find it a bit dull after London, I expect," he remarked, as he inserted his key in the door of a small house in a quiet street.

"I'm tired of London," said Miss Garland. "I think this is a beautiful little old town—so peaceful."

Mr. Mott looked gratified.

"I hope you'll stay a long time," he said, as he led the way into the small front room. "I'm a lonely old man."

His niece sank into an easy chair, and looked about her.

"Thank you," she said, slowly. "I hope I shall. I feel better already. There is so much to upset one in London."

"Noise?" queried Mr. Mott.

"And other things," said Miss Garland, with a slight shudder.

Mr. Mott sighed in sympathy with the unknown, and, judging by his niece's expression, the unknowable. He rearranged the teacups, and, going to the kitchen, returned in a few minutes with a pot of tea.

"Mrs. Pett leaves at three," he said, in explanation, "to look after her children, but she comes back again at eight to look after my supper. And how is your mother?"

Miss Garland told him.

"Last letter I had from her," said Mr. Mott, stealing a glance at the girl's ring-finger, "I understood you were engaged."

His niece drew herself up.

"Certainly not," she said, with considerable vigour. "I have seen too much of married life. I prefer my freedom. Besides, I don't like men."

Mr. Mott said modestly that he didn't wonder at it, and, finding the subject uncongenial, turned the conversation on to worthier subjects. Miss Garland's taste, it seemed, lay in the direction of hospital nursing, or some other occupation beneficial to mankind at large. Simple and demure, she filled the simpler Mr. Mott with a strong sense of the shortcomings of his unworthy sex.

Within two days, under the darkling glance of Mrs. Pett, she had altered the arrangements of the house. Flowers appeared on the meal-table, knives and forks were properly cleaned, and plates no longer appeared ornamented with the mustard of a previous meal. Fresh air circulated through the house, and, passing from Mrs. Pett's left knee to the lumbar region of Mr. Mott, went on its beneficent way rejoicing.

On the fifth day of her visit, Mr. Mott sat alone in the front parlour. The window was closed, the door was closed, and Mr. Mott, sitting in an easy chair with his feet up, was aroused from a sound nap by the door opening to admit a young man, who, deserted by Mrs. Pett, stood bowing awkwardly in the doorway.

"Is Miss Garland in?" he stammered.

Mr. Mott rubbed the remnants of sleep from his eyelids.

"She has gone for a walk," he said, slowly.

The young man stood fingering his hat.

"My name is Hurst," he said, with slight emphasis. "Mr. Alfred Hurst."

Mr. Mott, still somewhat confused, murmured that he was glad to hear it.

"I have come from London to see Florrie," continued the intruder. "I suppose she won't be long?"

Mr. Mott thought not, and after a moment's hesitation invited Mr. Hurst to take a chair.

"I suppose she told you we are engaged?" said the latter.

"Engaged!" said the startled Mr. Mott. "Why, she told me she didn't like men."

"Playfulness," replied Mr. Hurst, with an odd look. "Ah, here she is!"

The handle of the front door turned, and a moment later the door of the room was opened and the charming head of Miss Garland appeared in the opening.

"Back again," she said, brightly. "I've just been—"

She caught sight of Mr. Hurst, and the words died away on her lips. The door slammed, and the two gentlemen, exchanging glances, heard a hurried rush upstairs and the slamming of another door. Also a key was heard to turn sharply in a lock.

"She doesn't want to see you," said Mr. Mott, staring.

The young man turned pale.

"Perhaps she has gone upstairs to take her things off," he muttered, resuming his seat. "Don't— don't hurry her!"

"I wasn't going to," said Mr. Mott.

He twisted his beard uneasily, and at the end of ten minutes looked from the clock to Mr. Hurst and coughed.

"If you wouldn't mind letting her know I'm waiting," said the young man, brokenly.

Mr. Mott rose, and went slowly upstairs. More slowly still, after an interval of a few minutes, he came back again.

"She doesn't want to see you," he said, slowly.

Mr. Hurst gasped.

"I—I must see her," he faltered.

"She won't see you," repeated Mr. Mott. "And she told me to say she was surprised at you following her down here."

Mr. Hurst uttered a faint moan, and with bent head passed into the little passage and out into the street, leaving Mr. Mott to return to the sitting-room and listen to such explanations as Miss Garland deemed advisable. Great goodness of heart in the face of persistent and unwelcome attentions appeared to be responsible for the late engagement.

"Well, it's over now," said her uncle, kindly, "and no doubt he'll soon find somebody else. There are plenty of girls would jump at him, I expect."

Miss Garland shook her head.

"He said he couldn't live without me," she remarked, soberly.

Mr. Mott laughed.

"In less than three months I expect he'll be congratulating himself," he said, cheerfully. "Why, I was nearly cau—married, four times. It's a silly age."

His niece said "Indeed!" and, informing him in somewhat hostile tones that she was suffering from a severe headache, retired to her room.

Mr. Mott spent the evening by himself, and retiring to bed at ten-thirty was awakened by a persistent knocking at the front door at half-past one. Half awakened, he lit a candle, and, stumbling downstairs, drew back the bolt of the door, and stood gaping angrily at the pathetic features of Mr. Hurst.

"Sorry to disturb you," said the young man, "but would you mind giving this letter to Miss Garland?"

"Sorry to disturb me!" stuttered Mr. Mott. "What do you mean by it? Eh? What do you mean by it?"

"It is important," said Mr. Hurst. "I can't rest. I've eaten nothing all day."

"Glad to hear it," snapped the irritated Mr. Mott.

"If you will give her that letter, I shall feel easier," said Mr. Hurst.

"I'll give it to her in the morning," said the other, snatching it from him. "Now get off."

Mr. Hurst still murmuring apologies, went, and Mr. Mott, also murmuring, returned to bed. The night was chilly, and it was some time before he could get to sleep again. He succeeded at last, only to be awakened an hour later by a knocking more violent than before. In a state of mind bordering upon frenzy, he dived into his trousers again and went blundering downstairs in the dark.

"Sorry to—" began Mr. Hurst.

Mr. Mott made uncouth noises at him.

"I have altered my mind," said the young man. "Would you mind letting me have that letter back again? It was too final."

"You—get—off !" said the other, trembling with cold and passion.

"I must have that letter," said Mr. Hurst, doggedly. "All my future happiness may depend upon it."

Mr. Mott, afraid to trust himself with speech, dashed upstairs, and after a search for the matches found the letter, and, returning to the front door, shut it on the visitor's thanks. His niece's door opened as he passed it, and a gentle voice asked for enlightenment.

"How silly of him!" she said, softly. "I hope he won't catch cold. What did you say?"

"I was coughing," said Mr. Mott, hastily.

"You'll get cold if you're not careful," said his thoughtful niece. "That's the worst of men, they never seem to have any thought. Did he seem angry, or mournful, or what? I suppose you couldn't see his face?"

"I didn't try," said Mr. Mott, crisply. "Good night."

By the morning his ill-humour had vanished, and he even became slightly facetious over the events of the night. The mood passed at the same moment that Mr. Hurst passed the window.

"Better have him in and get it over," he said, irritably.

Miss Garland shuddered.

"Never!" she said, firmly. "He'd be down on his knees. It would be too painful. You don't know him."

"Don't want to," said Mr. Mott.

He finished his breakfast in silence, and, after a digestive pipe, proposed a walk. The profile of Mr. Hurst, as it went forlornly past the window again, served to illustrate Miss Garland's refusal.

"I'll go out and see him," said Mr. Mott, starting up. "Are you going to be a prisoner here until this young idiot chooses to go home? It's preposterous!"

He crammed his hat on firmly and set out in pursuit of Mr. Hurst, who was walking slowly up the street, glancing over his shoulder. "Morning!" said Mr. Mott, fiercely. "Good morning," said the other.

"Now, look here," said Mr. Mott. "This has gone far enough, and I won't have any more of it. Why, you ought to be ashamed of yourself, chivvying a young lady that doesn't want you. Haven't you got any pride?"

"No," said the young man, "not where she is concerned."

"I don't believe you have," said the other, regarding him, "and I expect that's where the trouble is. Did she ever have reason to think you were looking after any other girls?"

"Never, I swear it," said Mr. Hurst, eagerly.

"Just so," said Mr. Mott, with a satisfied nod. "That's where you made a mistake. She was too sure of you; it was too easy. No excitement. Girls like a man that other girls want; they don't want a turtle-dove in fancy trousers."

Mr. Hurst coughed.

"And they like a determined man," continued Miss Garland's uncle. "Why, in my young days, if I had been jilted, and come down to see about it, d'you think I'd have gone out of the house without seeing her? I might have been put out—by half-a-dozen—but I'd have taken the mantelpiece and a few other things with me. And you are bigger than I am."

"We aren't all made the same," said Mr. Hurst, feebly.

"No, we're not," said Mr. Mott. "I'm not blaming you; in a way, I'm sorry for you. If you're not born with a high spirit, nothing'll give it to you."

"It might be learnt," said Mr. Hurst. Mr. Mott laughed.

"High spirits are born, not made," he said. "The best thing you can do is to go and find another girl, and marry her before she finds you out."

Mr. Hurst shook his head.

"There's no other girl for me," he said, miserably. "And everything seemed to be going so well. We've been buying things for the house for the last six months, and I've just got a good rise in my screw."

"It'll do for another girl," said Mr. Mott, briskly. "Now, you get off back to town. You are worrying Florrie by staying here, and you are doing no good to anybody. Good-bye."

"I'll walk back as far as the door with you," said Mr. Hurst. "You've done me good. It's a pity I didn't meet you before."

"Remember what I've told you, and you'll do well yet," he said, patting the young man on the arm.

"I will," said Mr. Hurst, and walked on by his side, deep in thought.

"I can't ask you in," said Mr. Mott, jocularly, as he reached his door, and turned the key in the lock. "Good-bye."

"Good-bye," said Mr. Hurst.

He grasped the other's outstretched hand, and with a violent jerk pulled him into the street. Then he pushed open the door, and, slipping into the passage, passed hastily into the front room, closely followed by the infuriated Mr. Mott.

"What—what—what!" stammered that gentleman.

"I'm taking your tip," said Mr. Hurst, pale but determined. "I'm going to stay here until I have seen Florrie."

"You—you're a serpent," said Mr. Mott, struggling for breath. "I—I'm surprised at you. You go out before you get hurt."

"Not without the mantelpiece," said Mr. Hurst, with a distorted grin.

"A viper!" said Mr. Mott, with extreme bitterness. "If you are not out in two minutes I'll send for the police."

"Florrie wouldn't like that," said Mr. Hurst. "She's awfully particular about what people think. You just trot upstairs and tell her that a gentleman wants to see her."

He threw himself into Mr. Mott's own particular easy chair, and, crossing his knees, turned a deaf ear to the threats of that incensed gentleman. Not until the latter had left the room did his features reveal the timorousness of the soul within. Muffled voices sounded from upstairs, and it was evident that an argument of considerable length was in progress. It was also evident from the return of Mr. Mott alone that his niece had had the best of it.

"I've done all I could," he said, "but she declines to see you. She says she won't see you if you stay here for a month, and you couldn't do that, you know."

"Why not?" inquired Mr. Hurst.

"Why not?" repeated Mr. Mott, repressing his feelings with some difficulty. "Food!"

Mr. Hurst started.

"And drink," said Mr. Mott, following up his advantage. "There's no good in starving yourself for nothing, so you may as well go."

"When I've seen Florrie," said the young man, firmly.

Mr. Mott slammed the door, and for the rest of the day Mr. Hurst saw him no more. At one o'clock a savoury smell passed the door on its way upstairs, and at five o'clock a middle-aged woman with an inane smile looked into the room on her way aloft with a loaded tea-tray. By supper-time he was suffering considerably from hunger and thirst.

At ten o'clock he heard the footsteps of Mr. Mott descending the stairs. The door opened an inch, and a gruff voice demanded to know whether he was going to stay there all night. Receiving a cheerful reply in the affirmative, Mr. Mott secured the front door with considerable violence, and went off to bed without another word.

He was awakened an hour or two later by the sound of something falling, and, sitting up in bed to listen, became aware of a warm and agreeable odour. It was somewhere about the hour of midnight, but a breakfast smell of eggs and bacon would not be denied.

He put on some clothes and went downstairs. A crack of light showed under the kitchen door, and, pushing t open with some force, he gazed spellbound at the spectacle before him.

"Come in," said Mr. Hurst, heartily. "I've just finished."

He rocked an empty beer-bottle and patted another that was half full. Satiety was written on his face as he pushed an empty plate from him, and, leaning back in his chair, smiled lazily at Mr. Mott.

"Go on," said that gentleman, hoarsely. Mr. Hurst shook his head.

"Enough is as good as a feast," he said, reasonably. "I'll have some more to-morrow."

"Oh, will you?" said the other. "Will you?"

Mr. Hurst nodded, and, opening his coat, disclosed a bottle of beer in each breast-pocket. The other pockets, it appeared, contained food.

"And here's the money for it," he said, putting down some silver on the table. "I am determined, but honest."

With a sweep of his hand, Mr. Mott sent the money flying.

"To-morrow morning I send for the police. Mind that!" he roared.

"I'd better have my breakfast early, then," said Mr. Hurst, tapping his pockets. "Good night. And thank you for your advice."

He sat for some time after the disappearance of his host, and then, returning to the front room, placed a chair at the end of the sofa and, with the tablecloth for a quilt, managed to secure a few hours' troubled sleep. At eight o'clock he washed at the scullery sink, and at ten o'clock Mr. Mott, with an air of great determination, came in to deliver his ultimatum.

"If you're not outside the front door in five minutes, I'm going to fetch the police," he said, fiercely.

"I want to see Florrie," said the other.

"Well, you won't see her," shouted Mr. Mott.

Mr. Hurst stood feeling his chin.

"Well, would you mind taking a message for me?" he asked. "I just want you to ask her whether I am really free. Ask her whether I am free to marry again."

Mr. Mott eyed him in amazement.

"You see, I only heard from her mother," pursued Mr. Hurst, "and a friend of mine who is in a solicitor's office says that isn't good enough. I only came down here to make sure, and I think the least she can do is to tell me herself. If she won't see me, perhaps she'd put it in writing. You see, there's another lady."

"But" said the mystified Mr. Mott.

"You told me—"

"You tell her that," said the other.

Mr. Mott stood for a few seconds staring at him, and then without a word turned on his heel and went upstairs. Left to himself, Mr. Hurst walked nervously up and down the room, and, catching sight of his face in the old-fashioned glass on the mantel-piece, heightened its colour by a few pinches. The minutes seemed inter-minable, but at last he heard the steps of Mr. Mott on the stairs again.

"She's coming down to see you herself," said the latter, solemnly.

Mr. Hurst nodded, and, turning to the window, tried in vain to take an interest in passing events. A light step sounded on the stairs, the door creaked, and he turned to find himself con-fronted by Miss Garland.

"Uncle told me" she began, coldly. Mr. Hurst bowed.

"I am sorry to have caused you so much trouble," he said, trying to control his voice, "but you see my position, don't you?"

"No," said the girl.

"Well, I wanted to make sure," said Mr. Hurst. "It's best for all of us, isn't it? Best for you, best for me, and, of course, for my young lady."

"You never said anything about her before," said Miss Garland, her eyes darkening.

"Of course not," said Mr. Hurst. "How could I? I was engaged to you, and then she wasn't my young lady; but, of course, as soon as you broke it off—"

"Who is she?" inquired Miss Garland, in a casual voice.

"You don't know her," said Mr. Hurst.

"What is she like?"

"I can't describe her very well," said Mr. Hurst. "I can only say she's the most beautiful girl I have ever seen. I think that's what made me take to her. And she's easily pleased. She liked the things I have been buying for the house tremendously."

"Did she?" said Miss Garland, with a gasp.

"All except that pair of vases you chose," continued the veracious Mr. Hurst. "She says they are in bad taste, but she can give them to the charwoman."

"Oh!" said the girl. "Oh, indeed! Very kind of her. Isn't there anything else she doesn't like?"

Mr. Hurst stood considering.

"She doesn't like the upholstering of the best chairs," he said at last. "She thinks they are too showy, so she's going to put covers over them."

There was a long pause, during which Mr. Mott, taking his niece gently by the arm, assisted her to a chair.

"Otherwise she is quite satisfied," concluded Mr. Hurst.

Miss Garland took a deep breath, but made no reply.

"I have got to satisfy her that I am free," said the young man, after another pause. "I suppose that I can do so?"

"I—I'll think it over," said Miss Garland, in a low voice. "I am not sure what is the right thing to do. I don't want to see you made miserable for life. It's nothing to me, of course, but still—"

She got up and, shaking off the proffered assistance of her uncle, went slowly and languidly up to her room. Mr. Mott followed her as far as the door, and then turned indignantly upon Mr. Hurst.

"You—you've broke her heart," he said, solemnly.

"That's all right," said Mr. Hurst, with a delighted wink. "I'll mend it again."

THE MADNESS OF MR. LISTER

Old Jem Lister, of the *Susannah,* was possessed of two devils—the love of strong drink and avarice—and the only thing the twain had in common was to get a drink without paying for it. When Mr. Lister paid for a drink, the demon of avarice masquerading as conscience preached a teetotal lecture, and when he showed signs of profiting by it, the demon of drink would send him hanging round public-house doors cadging for drinks in a way which his shipmates regarded as a slur upon the entire ship's company. Many a healthy thirst reared on salt beef and tickled with strong tobacco had been spoiled by the sight of Mr. Lister standing by the entrance, with a propitiatory smile, waiting to be invited in to share it, and on one occasion they had even seen him (him, Jem Lister, A.B.) holding a horse's head, with ulterior motives.

It was pointed out to Mr. Lister at last that his conduct was reflecting discredit upon men who were fully able to look after themselves in that direction, without having any additional burden thrust upon them. Bill Henshaw was the spokesman, and on the score of violence (miscalled firmness) his remarks left little to be desired. On the score of profanity, Bill might recall with pride that in the opinion of his fellows he had left nothing unsaid.

"You ought to ha' been a member o' Parliament, Bill," said Harry Lea, when he had finished.

"It wants money," said Henshaw, shaking his head.

Mr. Lister laughed, a senile laugh, but not lacking in venom.

"That's what we've got to say," said Henshaw, turning upon him suddenly. "If there's anything I hate in this world, it's a drinking miser. You know our opinion, and the best thing you can do is to turn over a new leaf now."

"Take us all in to the Goat and Compasses," urged Lea; "bring out some o' those sovrins you've been hoarding."

Mr. Lister gazed at him with frigid scorn, and finding that the conversation still seemed to centre round his unworthy person, went up on deck and sat glowering over the insults which had been heaped upon him. His futile wrath when Bill dogged his footsteps ashore next day and revealed his character to a bibulous individual whom he had almost persuaded to be a Christian—from his point of view—bordered upon the maudlin, and he wandered back to the ship, wild-eyed and dry of throat.

For the next two months it was safe to say that every drink he had he paid for. His eyes got brighter and his complexion clearer, nor was he as pleased as one of the other sex might have been when the self-satisfied Henshaw pointed out these improvements to his companions, and claimed entire responsibility for them. It is probable that Mr. Lister, under these circumstances, might in time have lived down his taste for strong drink, but that at just that time they shipped a new cook.

He was a big, cadaverous young fellow, who looked too closely after his own interests to be much of a favourite with the other men forward. On the score of thrift, it was soon discovered that he and Mr. Lister had much in common, and the latter, pleased to find a congenial spirit, was disposed to make the most of him, and spent, despite the heat, much of his spare time in the galley.

"You keep to it," said the greybeard impressively; "money was made to be took care of; if you don't spend your money you've always got it. I've always been a saving man—what's the result?"

The cook, waiting some time in patience to be told, gently inquired what it was.

"'Ere am I," said Mr. Lister, good-naturedly helping him to cut a cabbage, "at the age of sixty-two with a bank-book down below in my chest, with one hundered an' ninety pounds odd in it."

"One 'undered and ninety pounds!" repeated the cook, with awe.

"To say nothing of other things," continued Mr. Lister, with joyful appreciation of the effect he was producing. "Altogether I've got a little over four 'undered pounds."

The cook gasped, and with gentle firmness took the cabbage from him as being unfit work for a man of such wealth.

"It's very nice," he said, slowly. "It's very nice. You'll be able to live on it in your old age."

Mr. Lister shook his head mournfully, and his eyes became humid.

"There's no old age for me," he said, sadly; "but you needn't tell them," and he jerked his thumb towards the forecastle.

"No, no," said the cook.

"I've never been one to talk over my affairs," said Mr. Lister, in a low voice. "I've never yet took fancy enough to anybody so to do. No, my lad, I'm saving up for somebody else."

"What are you going to live on when you're past work then?" demanded the other.

Mr. Lister took him gently by the sleeve, and his voice sank with the solemnity of his subject: "I'm not going to have no old age," he said, resignedly.

"Not going to live!" repeated the cook, gazing uneasily at a knife by his side. "How do you know?"

"I went to a orsepittle in London," said Mr. Lister. "I've been to two or three altogether, while the money I've spent on doctors is more than I like to think of, and they're all surprised to think that I've lived so long. I'm so chock-full o' complaints, that they tell me I can't live more than two years, and I might go off at any moment."

"Well, you've got money," said the cook, "why don't you knock off work now and spend the evenin' of your life ashore? Why should you save up for your relatives?"

"I've got no relatives," said Mr. Lister; "I'm all alone. I 'spose I shall leave my money to some nice young feller, and I hope it'll do 'im good."

With the dazzling thoughts which flashed through the cook's brain the cabbage dropped violently into the saucepan, and a shower of cooling drops fell on both men.

"I 'spose you take medicine?" he said, at length.

"A little rum," said Mr. Lister, faintly; "the doctors tell me that it is the only thing that keeps me up—o' course, the chaps down there "—he indicated the forecastle again with a jerk of his head—"accuse me o' taking too much."

"What do ye take any notice of 'em for?" inquired the other, indignantly.

"I 'spose it is foolish," admitted Mr. Lister; "but I don't like being misunderstood. I keep my troubles to myself as a rule, cook. I don't know what's made me talk to you like this. I 'eard the other day you was keeping company with a young woman."

"Well, I won't say as I ain't," replied the other, busying himself over the fire.

"An' the best thing, too, my lad," said the old man, warmly. "It keeps you stiddy, keeps you out of public-'ouses; not as they ain't good in moderation—I 'ope you'll be 'appy."

A friendship sprang up between the two men which puzzled the remainder of the crew not a little.

The cook thanked him, and noticed that Mr. Lister was fidgeting with a piece of paper.

"A little something I wrote the other day," said the old man, catching his eye. "If I let you see it, will you promise not to tell a soul about it, and not to give me no thanks?"

The wondering cook promised, and, the old man being somewhat emphatic on the subject, backed his promise with a home made affidavit of singular power and profanity.

"Here it is, then," said Mr. Lister.

The cook took the paper, and as he read the letters danced before him. He blinked his eyes and started again, slowly. In plain black and white and nondescript-coloured finger-marks, Mr. Lister, after a general statement as to his bodily and mental health, left the whole of his estate to the cook. The will was properly dated and witnessed, and the cook's voice shook with excitement and emotion as he offered to hand it back.

"I don't know what I've done for you to do this," he said.

Mr. Lister waved it away again. "Keep it," he said, simply; "while you've got it on you, you'll know it's safe."

From this moment a friendship sprang up between the two men which puzzled the remainder of the crew not a little. The attitude of the cook was as that of a son to a father: the benignancy of Mr. Lister beautiful to behold. It was noticed, too, that he had abandoned the reprehensible practice of hanging round tavern doors in favour of going inside and drinking the cook's health.

For about six months the cook, although always in somewhat straitened circumstances, was well content with the tacit bargain, and then, bit by bit, the character of Mr. Lister was revealed to him. It was not a nice character, but subtle; and when he made the startling discovery that a will could be rendered invalid by the simple process of making another one the next day, he became as a man possessed. When he ascertained that Mr. Lister when at home had free quarters at the house of a married niece, he used to sit about alone, and try and think of ways and means of securing capital sunk in a concern which seemed to show no signs of being wound-up.

"I've got a touch of the 'art again, lad," said the elderly invalid, as they sat alone in the forecastle one night at Seacole.

"You move about too much," said the cook. "Why not turn in and rest?"

Mr. Lister, who had not expected this, fidgeted. "I think I'll go ashore a bit and try the air," he said, suggestively. "I'll just go as far as the Black Horse and back. You won't have me long now, my lad."

"No, I know," said the cook; "that's what's worrying me a bit." "Don't worry about me," said the old man, pausing with his hand on the other's shoulder; "I'm not worth it. Don't look so glum, lad."

"I've got something on my mind, Jem," said the cook, staring straight in front of him.

"What is it?" inquired Mr. Lister.

"You know what you told me about those pains in your inside?" said the cook, without looking at him.

Jem groaned and felt his side.

"And what you said about its being a relief to die," continued the other, "only you was afraid to commit suicide?"

"Well?" said Mr. Lister.

"It used to worry me," continued the cook, earnestly. "I used to say to myself, 'Poor old Jem,' I ses, 'why should 'e suffer like this when he wants to die? It seemed 'ard.'"

"It is 'ard," said Mr. Lister, "but what about it?"

The other made no reply, but looking at him for the first time, surveyed him with a troubled expression.

"What about it?" repeated Mr. Lister, with some emphasis.

"You did say you wanted to die, didn't you?" said the cook. "Now suppose suppose—"

"Suppose what?" inquired the old man, sharply. "Why don't you say what you're agoing to say?"

"Suppose," said the cook, "some one what liked you, Jem—what liked you, mind—'eard you say this over and over again, an' see you sufferin' and 'eard you groanin' and not able to do nothin' for you except lend you a few shillings here and there for medicine, or stand you a few glasses o' rum; suppose they knew a chap in a chemist's shop?"

"Suppose they did?" said the other, turning pale.

"A chap what knows all about p'isons," continued the cook, "p'isons what a man can take without knowing it in 'is grub. Would it be wrong, do you think, if that friend I was speaking about put it in your food to put you out of your misery?"

"Wrong," said Mr. Lister, with glassy eyes. "Wrong. Look 'ere, cook—"

"I don't mean anything to give him pain," said the other, waving his hand; "you ain't felt no pain lately, 'ave you, Jem?"

"Do you mean to say" shouted Mr. Lister.

"I don't mean to say anything," said the cook. "Answer my question. You ain't felt no pain lately, 'ave you?"

"Have—you—been—putting—p'ison—in—my—wittles?" demanded Mr. Lister, in trembling accents.

"If I 'ad, Jem, supposin' that I 'ad," said the cook, in accents of reproachful surprise, "do you mean to say that you'd mind?"

"MIND," said Mr. Lister, with fervour. "I'd 'ave you 'ung!"

"But you said you wanted to die," said the surprised cook.

Mr. Lister swore at him with startling vigour. "I'll 'ave you 'ung," he repeated, wildly.

"Me," said the cook, artlessly. "What for?"

"For giving me p'ison," said Mr. Lister, frantically. "Do you think you can deceive me by your roundabouts? Do you think I can't see through you?"

The other with a sphinx-like smile sat unmoved. "Prove it," he said, darkly. "But supposin' if anybody 'ad been givin' you p'ison, would you like to take something to prevent its acting?"

"I'd take gallons of it," said Mr. Lister, feverishly.

The other sat pondering, while the old man watched him anxiously. "It's a pity you don't know your own mind, Jem," he said, at length; "still, you know your own business best. But it's very expensive stuff."

"How much?" inquired the other.

"Well, they won't sell more than two shillings-worth at a time," said the cook, trying to speak carelessly, "but if you like to let me 'ave the money, I'll go ashore to the chemist's and get the first lot now."

Mr. Lister's face was a study in emotions, which the other tried in vain to decipher.

Then he slowly extracted the amount from his trousers-pocket, and handed it over with-out a word.

"I'll go at once," said the cook, with a little feeling, "and I'll never take a man at his word again, Jem."

He ran blithely up on deck, and stepping ashore, spat on the coins for luck and dropped them in his pocket. Down below, Mr. Lister, with his chin in his hand, sat in a state of mind pretty evenly divided between rage and fear.

The cook, who was in no mood for company, missed the rest of the crew by two public-houses, and having purchased a baby's teething powder and removed the label, had a congratulatory drink or two before going on board again. A chatter of voices from the forecastle warned him that the crew had returned, but the tongues ceased abruptly as he descended, and three pairs of eyes surveyed him in grim silence.

"What's up?" he demanded.

"Wot 'ave you been doin' to poor old Jem?" demanded Henshaw, sternly.

"Nothin'," said the other, shortly.

"You ain't been p'isoning 'im?" demanded Henshaw.

"Certainly not," said the cook, emphatically.

"He ses you told 'im you p'isoned 'im," said Henshaw, solemnly, "and 'e give you two shillings to get something to cure 'im. It's too late now."

"What?" stammered the bewildered cook. He looked round anxiously at the men.

They were all very grave, and the silence became oppressive. "Where is he?" he demanded.

Henshaw and the others exchanged glances. "He's gone mad," said he, slowly.

"Mad?" repeated the horrified cook, and, seeing the aversion of the crew, in a broken voice he narrated the way in which he had been victimized.

"Well, you've done it now," said Henshaw, when he had finished. "He's gone right orf 'is 'ed."

"Where is he?" inquired the cook.

"Where you can't follow him," said the other, slowly.

"Heaven?" hazarded the unfortunate cook. "No; skipper's bunk," said Lea.

"Oh, can't I foller 'im?" said the cook, starting up. "I'll soon 'ave 'im out o' that."

"Better leave 'im alone," said Henshaw. "He was that wild we couldn't do nothing with 'im, singing an' larfin' and crying all together—I certainly thought he was p'isoned."

"I'll swear I ain't touched him," said the cook.

"Well, you've upset his reason," said Henshaw; "there'll be an awful row when the skipper comes aboard and finds 'im in 'is bed.

"'Well, come an' 'elp me to get 'im out," said the cook.

"I ain't going to be mixed up in it," said Henshaw, shaking his head.

"Don't you, Bill," said the other two.

"Wot the skipper'll say I don't know," said Henshaw; "anyway, it'll be said to you, not—"

"I'll go and get 'im out if 'e was five madmen," said the cook, compressing his lips.

"You'll harve to carry 'im out, then," said Henshaw. "I don't wish you no 'arm, cook, and perhaps it would be as well to get 'im out afore the skipper or mate comes aboard. If it was me, I know what I should do."

"What?" inquired the cook, breathlessly.

"Draw a sack over his head," said Henshaw, impressively; "he'll scream like blazes as soon as you touch him, and rouse the folks ashore if you don't. Besides that, if you draw it well down it'll keep his arms fast."

The cook thanked him fervently, and routing out a sack, rushed hastily on deck, his departure being the signal for Mr. Henshaw and his friends to make preparations for retiring for the night so hastily as almost to savour of panic.

The cook, after a hasty glance ashore, went softly below with the sack over his arm and felt his way in the darkness to the skipper's bunk. The sound of deep and regular breathing reassured him, and without undue haste he opened the mouth of the sack and gently raised the sleeper's head.

"Eh? Wha—" began a sleepy voice.

The next moment the cook had bagged him, and gripping him tightly round the middle, turned a deaf ear to the smothered cries of his victim as he strove to lift him out of the bunk. In the exciting time which followed, he had more than one reason for thinking that he had caught a centipede.

"Now, you keep still," he cried, breathlessly. "I'm not going to hurt you."

He got his burden out of bed at last, and staggered to the foot of the companion-ladder with it. Then there was a halt, two legs sticking obstinately across the narrow way and refusing to be moved, while a furious humming proceeded from the other end of the sack.

Four times did the exhausted cook get his shoulder under his burden and try and push it up the ladder, and four times did it wriggle and fight its way down again. Half crazy with fear and rage, he essayed it for the fifth time, and had got it half-way up when there was a sudden exclamation of surprise from above, and the voice of the mate sharply demanding an explanation.

"What the blazes are you up to?" he cried.

"It's all right, sir," said the panting cook; "old Jem's had a drop too much and got down aft, and I'm getting 'im for'ard again."

"Jem?" said the astonished mate. "Why, he's sitting up here on the fore-hatch. He came aboard with me."

"Sitting," began the horrified cook; "sit—oh, lor!"

He stood with his writhing burden wedged between his body and the ladder, and looked up despairingly at the mate.

"I'm afraid I've made a mistake," he said in a trembling voice.

The mate struck a match and looked down.

"Take that sack off," he demanded, sternly.

The cook placed his burden upon its feet, and running up the ladder stood by the mate shivering. The latter struck another match, and the twain watched in breathless silence the writhings of the strange creature below as the covering worked slowly upwards. In the fourth match it got free, and revealed the empurpled visage of the master of the *Susannah*. For the fraction of a second the cook gazed at him in speechless horror, and then, with a hopeless cry, sprang ashore and ran for it, hotly pursued by his enraged victim. At the time of sailing he was still absent, and the skipper, loth to part two such friends, sent Mr. James Lister, at the urgent request of the anxious crew, to look for him.

The night-watchman appeared to be out of sorts. His movements were even slower than usual, and, when he sat, the soap-box seemed to be unable to give satisfaction. His face bore an expression of deep melancholy, but a smouldering gleam in his eye betokened feelings deeply moved.

"Play-acting I don't hold with," he burst out, with sudden ferocity. "Never did. I don't say I ain't been to a theayter once or twice in my life, but I always come away with the idea that anybody could act if they liked to try. It's a kid's game, a silly kid's game, dressing up and pretending to be somebody else."

He cut off a piece of tobacco and, stowing it in his left cheek, sat chewing, with his lack-lustre eyes fixed on the wharves across the river. The offensive antics of a lighterman in mid-stream, who nearly fell overboard in his efforts to attract his attention, he ignored.

"I might ha' known it, too," he said, after a long silence. "If I'd only stopped to think, instead o' being in such a hurry to do good to others, I should ha' been all right, and the pack o' monkey-faced swabs on the *Lizzie and Annie* wot calls themselves sailor-men would 'ave had to 'ave got something else to laugh about. They've told it in every pub for 'arf a mile round, and last night, when I went into the Town of Margate to get a drink, three chaps climbed over the partition to 'ave a look at me.

"It all began with young Ted Sawyer, the mate o' the *Lizzie and Annie*. He calls himself a mate, but if it wasn't for 'aving the skipper for a brother-in-law 'e'd be called something else, very quick. Two or three times we've 'ad words over one thing and another, and the last time I called 'im something that I can see now was a mistake. It was one o' these 'ere clever things that a man don't forget, let alone a lop-sided monkey like 'im.

"That was when they was up time afore last, and when they made fast 'ere last week I could see as he 'adn't forgotten it. For one thing he pretended not to see me, and, arter I 'ad told him wot I'd do to him if 'e ran into me agin, he said 'e thought I was a sack o' potatoes taking a airing on a pair of legs wot somebody 'ad throwed away. Nasty tongue 'e's got; not clever, but nasty.

"Arter that I took no notice of 'im, and, o' course, that annoyed 'im more than anything. All I could do I done, and 'e was ringing the gate-bell that night from five minutes to twelve till ha'-past afore I heard it. Many a night-watchman gets a name for going to sleep when 'e's only getting a bit of 'is own back.

"We stood there talking for over 'arf-an-hour arter I 'ad let 'im in. Leastways, he did. And whenever I see as he was getting tired I just said, 'H'sh!' and 'e'd start agin as fresh as ever. He tumbled to it at last, and went aboard shaking 'is little fist at me and telling me wot he'd do to me if it wasn't for the lor.

"I kept by the gate as soon as I came on dooty next evening, just to give 'im a little smile as 'e went out. There is nothing more aggravating than a smile when it is properly done; but there was no signs o' my lord, and, arter practising it on a carman by mistake, I 'ad to go inside for a bit and wait till he 'ad gorn.

"The coast was clear by the time I went back, and I 'ad just stepped outside with my back up agin the gate-post to 'ave a pipe, when I see a boy coming along with a bag. Good-looking lad of about fifteen 'e was, nicely dressed in a serge suit, and he no sooner gets up to me than 'e puts down the bag and looks up at me with a timid sort o' little smile.

"'Good evening, cap'n,' he ses.

"He wasn't the fust that has made that mistake; older people than 'im have done it.

"'Good evening, my lad,' I ses.

"'I s'pose,' he ses, in a trembling voice, 'I suppose you ain't looking out for a cabin-boy, sir?'

"'Cabin-boy?' I ses. 'No, I ain't.'

"'I've run away from 'ome to go to sea,' he ses, and I'm afraid of being pursued. Can I come inside?'

"Afore I could say 'No' he 'ad come, bag and all; and afore I could say anything else he 'ad nipped into the office and stood there with his 'and on his chest panting.

"'I know I can trust you,' he ses; 'I can see it by your face.'

"'Wot 'ave you run away from 'ome for?' I ses. 'Have they been ill-treating of you?'

"'Ill-treating me?' he ses, with a laugh. 'Not much. Why, I expect my father is running about all over the place offering rewards for me. He wouldn't lose me for a thousand pounds.'

"I pricked up my ears at that; I don't deny it. Anybody would. Besides, I knew it would be doing him a kindness to hand 'im back to 'is father. And then I did a bit o' thinking to see 'ow it was to be done.

"'Sit down,' I ses, putting three or four ledgers on the floor behind one of the desks. 'Sit down, and let's talk it over.'

"We talked away forever so long, but, do all I would, I couldn't persuade 'im. His 'ead was stuffed full of coral islands and smugglers and pirates and foreign ports. He said 'e wanted to see the world, and flying-fish.

"'I love the blue billers,' he ses; 'the heaving blue billers is wot I want.'

"I tried to explain to 'im who would be doing the heaving, but 'e wouldn't listen to me. He sat on them ledgers like a little wooden image, looking up at me and shaking his 'ead, and when I told 'im of storms and shipwrecks he just smacked 'is lips and his blue eyes shone with joy. Arter a time I saw it was no good trying to persuade 'im, and I pretended to give way.

"'I think I can get you a ship with a friend o' mine,' I ses; 'but, mind, I've got to relieve your pore father's mind—I must let 'im know wot's become of you.'

"'Not before I've sailed,' he ses, very quick.

"'Certingly not,' I ses. 'But you must give me 'is name and address, and, arter the Blue Shark—that's the name of your ship—is clear of the land, I'll send 'im a letter with no name to it, saying where you ave gorn.'

"He didn't seem to like it at fust, and said 'e would write 'imself, but arter I 'ad pointed out that 'e might forget and that I was responsible, 'e gave way and told me that 'is father was named Mr. Watson, and he kept a big draper's shop in the Commercial Road.

"We talked a bit arter that, just to stop 'is suspicions, and then I told 'im to stay where 'e was on the floor, out of sight of the window, while I went to see my friend the captain.

"I stood outside for a moment trying to make up my mind wot to do. O'course, I 'ad no business, strictly speaking, to leave the wharf, but, on the other 'and, there was a father's 'art to relieve. I edged along bit by bit while I was thinking, and then, arter looking back once or twice to make sure that the boy wasn't watching me, I set off for the Commercial Road as hard as I could go.

"I'm not so young as I was. It was a warm evening, and I 'adn't got even a bus fare on me. I 'ad to walk all the way, and, by the time I got there, I was 'arf melted. It was a tidy-sized shop, with three or four nice-looking gals behind the counter, and things like babies' high chairs for the customers to sit onlong in the leg and ridikerlously small in the seat. I went up to one of the gals and told Per I wanted to see Mr. Watson.

"'On private business,' I ses. 'Very important.'

"She looked at me for a moment, and then she went away and fetched a tall, bald-headed man with grey side-whiskers and a large nose.

"'Wot d'you want?" he ses, coming up to me.

I want a word with you in private,' I ses.

"'This is private enough for me,' he ses. 'Say wot you 'ave to say, and be quick about it.'

"I drawed myself up a bit and looked at him. 'P'r'aps you ain't missed 'im yet,' I ses.

"'Missed 'im?' he ses, with a growl. 'Missed who?'

"'Your-son. Your blue-eyed son,' I ses, looking 'im straight in the eye.

"'Look here!' he ses, spluttering. 'You be off. 'Ow dare you come here with your games? Wot d'ye mean by it?'

"'I mean,' I ses, getting a bit out o' temper, 'that your boy has run away to go to sea, and I've come to take you to 'im.'

"He seemed so upset that I thought 'e was going to 'ave a fit at fust, and it seemed only natural, too. Then I see that the best-looking girl and another was having a fit, although trying 'ard not to.

"'If you don't get out o' my shop,' he ses at last, 'I'll 'ave you locked up.'

"'Very good!' I ses, in a quiet way. 'Very good; but, mark my words, if he's drownded you'll never forgive yourself as long as you live for letting your temper get the better of you—you'll never know a good night's rest agin. Besides, wot about 'is mother?'

"One o' them silly gals went off agin just like a damp firework, and Mr. Watson, arter nearly choking 'imself with temper, shoved me out o' the way and marched out o' the shop. I didn't know wot to make of 'im at fust, and then one o' the gals told me that 'e was a bachelor and 'adn't got no son, and that somebody 'ad been taking advantage of what she called my innercence to pull my leg.

"'You toddle off 'ome,' she ses, 'before Mr. Watson comes back.'

"'It's a shame to let 'im come out alone,' ses one o' the other gals. 'Where do you live, gran'pa?'

"I see then that I 'ad been done, and I was just walking out o' the shop, pretending to be deaf, when Mr. Watson come back with a silly young policeman wot asked me wot I meant by it. He told me to get off 'ome quick, and actually put his 'and on my shoulder, but it 'ud take more than a thing like that to push me, and, arter trying his 'ardest, he could only rock me a bit.

"I went at last because I wanted to see that boy agin, and the young policeman follered me quite a long way, shaking his silly 'ead at me and telling me to be careful.

"I got a ride part o' the way from Commercial Road to Aldgate by getting on the wrong bus, but it wasn't much good, and I was quite tired by the time I got back to the wharf. I waited outside for a minute or two to get my wind back agin, and then I went in-boiling.

"You might ha' knocked me down with a feather, as the saying is, and I just stood inside the office speechless. The boy 'ad disappeared and sitting on the floor where I 'ad left 'im was a very nice-looking gal of about eighteen, with short 'air, and a white blouse.

"'Good evening, sir,' she ses, jumping up and giving me a pretty little frightened look. 'I'm so sorry that my brother has been deceiving you. He's a bad, wicked, ungrateful boy. The idea of telling you that Mr. Watson was 'is father! Have you been there? I do 'ope you're not tired.'

"'Where is he?' I ses.

"'He's gorn,' she ses, shaking her 'ead. 'I begged and prayed of 'im to stop, but 'e wouldn't. He said 'e thought you might be offended with 'im. "Give my love to old Roley-Poley, and tell him I don't trust 'im," he ses.'

"She stood there looking so scared that I didn't know wot to say. By and by she took out 'er little pocket-'ankercher and began to cry—

"'Oh, get 'im back,' she ses. 'Don't let it be said I follered 'im 'ere all the way for nothing. Have another try. For my sake!'

"'Ow can I get 'im back when I don't know where he's gorn?' I ses.

"'He-he's gorn to 'is godfather,' she ses, dabbing her eyes. 'I promised 'im not to tell anybody; but I don't know wot to do for the best.'

"'Well, p'r'aps his godfather will 'old on to 'im,' I ses.

"'He won't tell 'im anything about going to sea,' she ses, shaking 'er little head. 'He's just gorn to try and bo—bo-borrow some money to go away with.'

"She bust out sobbing, and it was all I could do to get the godfather's address out of 'er. When I think of the trouble I took to get it I come over quite faint. At last she told me, between 'er sobs, that 'is name was Mr. Kiddem, and that he lived at 27, Bridge Street.

"'He's one o' the kindest-'arted and most generous men that ever lived,' she ses; 'that's why my brother Harry 'as gone to 'im. And you needn't mind taking anything 'e likes to give you; he's rolling in money.'

"I took it a bit easier going to Bridge Street, but the evening seemed 'otter than ever, and by the time I got to the 'ouse I was pretty near done up. A nice, tidy-looking woman opened the door, but she was a' most stone deaf, and I 'ad to shout the name pretty near a dozen times afore she 'eard it.

"'He don't live 'ere,' she ses.

"'As he moved?' I ses. 'Or wot?'

"She shook her 'cad, and, arter telling me to wait, went in and fetched her 'usband.

"'Never 'eard of him,' he ses, 'and we've been 'ere seventeen years. Are you sure it was twenty-seven?'

"'Sartain,' I ses.

"'Well, he don't live 'ere,' he ses. 'Why not try thirty-seven and forty-seven?'

"I tried 'em: thirty-seven was empty, and a pasty-faced chap at forty-seven nearly made 'imself ill over the name of 'Kiddem.' It 'adn't struck me before, but it's a hard matter to deceive me, and all in a flash it come over me that I 'ad been done agin, and that the gal was as bad as 'er brother.

"I was so done up I could 'ardly crawl back, and my 'ead was all in a maze. Three or four times I stopped and tried to think, but couldn't, but at last I got back and dragged myself into the office.

"As I 'arf expected, it was empty. There was no sign of either the gal or the boy; and I dropped into a chair and tried to think wot it all meant. Then, 'appening to look out of the winder, I see somebody running up and down the jetty.

"I couldn't see plain owing to the things in the way, but as soon as I got outside and saw who it was I nearly dropped. It was the boy, and he was running up and down wringing his 'ands and crying like a wild thing, and, instead o' running away as soon as 'e saw me, he rushed right up to me and threw 'is grubby little paws round my neck.

"'Save her!' 'e ses. 'Save 'er! Help! Help!'

"'Look 'ere,' I ses, shoving 'im off.

"'She fell overboard,' he ses, dancing about. 'Oh, my pore sister! Quick! Quick! I can't swim!'

"He ran to the side and pointed at the water, which was just about at 'arf-tide. Then 'e caught 'old of me agin.

"'Make 'aste,' he ses, giving me a shove behind. 'Jump in. Wot are you waiting for?'

"I stood there for a moment 'arf dazed, looking down at the water. Then I pulled down a life-belt from the wall 'ere and threw it in, and, arter another moment's thought, ran back to the *Lizzie and Annie,* wot was in the inside berth, and gave them a hail. I've always 'ad a good voice, and in a flash the skipper and Ted Sawyer came tumbling up out of the cabin and the 'ands out of the fo'c'sle.

"'Gal overboard!' I ses, shouting.

"The skipper just asked where, and then 'im and the mate and a couple of 'ands tumbled into their boat and pulled under the jetty for all they was worth. Me and the boy ran back and stood with the others, watching.

"'Point out the exact spot,' ses the skipper.

"The boy pointed, and the skipper stood up in the boat and felt round with a boat-hook. Twice 'e said he thought 'e touched something, but it turned out as 'e was mistaken. His face got longer and longer and 'e shook his 'ead, and said he was afraid it was no good.

"'Don't stand cryin' 'ere,' he ses to the boy, kindly. 'Jem, run round for the Thames police, and get them and the drags. Take the boy with you. It'll occupy 'is mind.'

"He 'ad another go with the boat-hook arter they 'ad gone; then 'e gave it up, and sat in the boat waiting.

"'This'll be a bad job for you, watchman,' he ses, shaking his 'ead. 'Where was you when it 'appened?'

"'He's been missing all the evening,' ses the cook, wot was standing beside me. 'If he'd been doing 'is dooty, the pore gal wouldn't 'ave been drownded. Wot was she doing on the wharf?'

"'Skylarkin', I s'pose,' ses the mate. 'It's a wonder there ain't more drownded. Wot can you expect when the watchman is sitting in a pub all the evening?'

"The cook said I ought to be 'ung, and a young ordinary seaman wot was standing beside 'im said he would sooner I was boiled. I believe they 'ad words about it, but I was feeling too upset to take much notice.

"'Looking miserable won't bring 'er back to life agin,' ses the skipper, looking up at me and shaking his 'ead. 'You'd better go down to my cabin and get yourself a drop o' whisky; there's a bottle on the table. You'll want all your wits about you when the police come. And wotever you do don't say nothing to criminate yourself.'

"'We'll do the criminating for 'im all right,' ses the cook.

"'If I was the pore gal I'd haunt 'im,' ses the ordinary seaman; 'every night of 'is life I'd stand afore 'im dripping with water and moaning.'

"'P'r'aps she will,' ses the cook; 'let's 'ope so, at any rate.'

"I didn't answer 'em; I was too dead-beat. Besides which, I've got a 'orror of ghosts, and the idea of being on the wharf alone of a night arter such a thing was a'most too much for me. I went on board the *Lizzie and Annie,* and down in the cabin I found a bottle o' whisky, as the skipper 'ad said. I sat down on the locker and 'ad a glass, and then I sat worrying and wondering wot was to be the end of it all.

"The whisky warmed me up a bit, and I 'ad just taken up the bottle to 'elp myself agin when I 'eard a faint sort o' sound in the skipper's state-room. I put the bottle down and listened, but everything seemed deathly still. I took it up agin, and 'ad just poured out a drop o' whisky when I distinctly 'eard a hissing noise and then a little moan.

"For a moment I sat turned to stone. Then I put the bottle down quiet, and 'ad just got up to go when the door of the state-room opened, and I saw the drownded gal, with 'er little face and hair all wet and dripping, standing before me.

"Ted Sawyer 'as been telling everybody that I came up the companion-way like a fog-horn that 'ad lost its ma; I wonder how he'd 'ave come up if he'd 'ad the evening I had 'ad?

"They were all on the jetty as I got there and tumbled into the skipper's arms, and all asking at once wot was the matter. When I got my breath back a bit and told 'em, they laughed. All except the cook, and 'e said it was only wot I might expect. Then, like a man in a dream, I see the gal come out of the companion and walk slowly to the side.

"'Look!' I ses. 'Look. There she is!'

"'You're dreaming,' ses the skipper, 'there's nothing there.'

"They all said the same, even when the gal stepped on to the side and climbed on to the wharf. She came along towards me with 'er arms held close to 'er sides, and making the most 'orrible faces at me, and it took five of'em all their time to 'old me. The wharf and everything seemed to me to spin round and round. Then she came straight up to me and patted me on the cheek.

"'Pore old gentleman,' she ses. 'Wot a shame it is, Ted! It's too bad.'

"They let go o' me then, and stamped up and down the jetty laughing fit to kill themselves. If they 'ad only known wot a exhibition they was making of themselves, and 'ow I pitied them, they wouldn't ha' done it. And by and by Ted wiped his eyes and put his arm round the gal's waist and ses—

"'This is my intended, Miss Florrie Price,' he ses. 'Ain't she a little wonder? Wot d'ye think of 'er?'

"'I'll keep my own opinion,' I ses. 'I ain't got nothing to say against gals, but if I only lay my hands on that young brother of 'ers'

"They went off agin then, worse than ever; and at last the cook came and put 'is skinny arm round my neck and started spluttering in my ear. I shoved 'im off hard, because I see it all then; and I should ha' seen it afore only I didn't 'ave time to think. I don't bear no malice, and all I can say is that I don't wish 'er any harder punishment than to be married to Ted Sawyer."

The schooner Falcon was ready for sea. The last bale of general cargo had just been shipped, and a few hairy, unkempt seamen were busy putting on the hatches under the able profanity of the mate.

"All clear?" inquired the master, a short, ruddy-faced man of about thirty-five. "Cast off there!"

"Ain't you going to wait for the passengers, then?" inquired the mate.

"No, no," replied the skipper, whose features were working with excitement. "They won't come now, I'm sure they won't. We'll lose the tide if we don't look sharp."

He turned aside to give an order just as a buxom young woman, accompanied by a loutish boy, a band-box, and several other bundles, came hurrying on to the jetty.

"Well, here we are, Cap'n Evans," said the girl, springing lightly on to the deck. "I thought we should never get here; the cabman didn't seem to know the way; but I knew you wouldn't go without us,"

"Here you are," said the skipper, with attempted cheerfulness, as he gave the girl his right hand, while his left strayed vaguely in the direction of the boy's ear, which was coldly withheld from him. "Go down below, and the mate'll show you your cabin. Bill, this is Miss Cooper, a lady friend o' mine, and her brother."

The mate, acknowledging the introduction, led the way to the cabin, where they remained so long that by the time they came on deck again the schooner was off Limehouse, slipping along well under a light wind.

"How do you like the state-room?" inquired the skipper, who was at the wheel.

"Pretty fair," replied Miss Cooper. "It's a big name for it though, ain't it? Oh, what a large ship!"

She ran to the side to gaze at a big liner, and as far as Gravesend besieged the skipper and mate with questions concerning the various craft. At the mate's suggestion they had tea on deck, at which meal William Henry Cooper became a source of much discomfort to his host by his remarkable discoveries anent the fauna of lettuce. Despite his efforts, however, and the cloud under which Evans seemed to be labouring, the meal was voted a big success; and after it was over they sat laughing and chatting until the air got chilly, and the banks of the river were lost in the gathering darkness. At ten o'clock they retired for the night, leaving Evans and the mate on deck.

"Nice gal, that," said the mate, looking at the skipper, who was leaning moodily on the wheel.

"Ay, ay," replied he. "Bill," he continued, turning suddenly towards the mate. "I'm in a deuce of a mess. You've got a good square head on your shoulders. Now, what on earth am I to do? Of course you can see how the land lays?"

"Of course," said the mate, who was not going to lose his reputation by any display of ignorance. "Anyone could see it," he added.

"The question is what's to be done?" said the skipper.

"That's the question," said the mate guardedly.

"I feel that worried," said Evans, "that I've actually thought of getting into collision, or running the ship ashore. Fancy them two women meeting at Llandalock."

Such a sudden light broke in upon the square head of the mate, that he nearly whistled with the brightness of it.

"But you ain't engaged to this one?" he cried.

"We're to be married in August," said the skipper desperately. "That's my ring on her finger."

"But you're going to marry Mary Jones in September," expostulated the mate. "You can't marry both of 'em."

"That's what I say," replied Evans; "that's what I keep telling myself, but it don't seem to bring much comfort I'm too soft-'earted where wimmen is concerned, Bill, an' that's the truth of it. D'reckly I get alongside of a nice gal my arm goes creeping round her before I know what it's doing."

"What on earth made you bring the girl on the ship?" inquired the mate. "The other one's sure to be on the quay to meet you as usual."

"I couldn't help it," groaned the skipper; "she would come; she can be very determined when she likes. She's awful gone on me, Bill."

"So's the other one apparently," said the mate.

"I can't think what it is the gals see in me," said the other mournfully. "Can you?"

"No, I'm blamed if I can," replied the mate frankly.

"I don't take no credit for it, Bill," said the skipper, "not a bit. My father was like it before me. The worry's killing me."

"Well, which are you going to have?" inquired the mate. "Which do you like the best?"

"I don't know, an' that's a fact," said the skipper. "They 've both got money coming to 'em; when I'm in Wales I like Mary Jones best, and when I'm in London it's Janey Cooper. It's dreadful to be like that, Bill."

"It is," said the mate drily. "I wouldn't be in your shoes when those two gals meet for a fortune. Then you'll have old Jones and her brothers to tackle, too. Seems to me things'll be a bit lively."

"I hev thought of being took sick, and staying in my bunk, Bill," suggested Evans anxiously.

"An' having the two of 'em to nurse you," retorted Bill. "Nice quiet time for an invalid."

Evans made a gesture of despair.

"How would it be," said the mate, after a long pause, and speaking very slowly; "how would it be if I took this one off your hands."

"You couldn't do it, Bill," said the skipper decidedly. "Not while she knew I was above ground."

"Well, I can try," returned the mate shortly. "I've took rather a fancy to the girl. Is it a bargain?"

"It is," said the skipper, shaking hands upon it. "If you git me out of this hole, Bill, I'll remember it the longest day I live."

With these words he went below, and, after cautiously undoing W. H. Cooper, who had slept himself into a knot that a professional contortionist would have envied, tumbled in beside him and went to sleep.

His heart almost failed him when he encountered the radiant Jane at breakfast in the morning, but he concealed his feelings by a strong effort; and after the meal was finished, and the passengers had gone on deck, he laid hold of the mate, who was following, and drew him into the cabin.

"You haven't washed yourself this morning," he said, eyeing him closely. "How do you s'pose you are going to make an impression if you don't look smart?"

"Well, I look tidier than you do," growled the mate.

"Of course you do," said the wily Evans. "I'm going to give you all the chances I can. Now you go and shave yourself, and here—take it."

He passed the surprised mate a brilliant red silk tie, embellished with green spots.

"No, no," said the mate deprecatingly.

"Take it," repeated Evans; "if anything'll fetch her it'll be that tie; and here's a couple of collars for you; they're a new shape, quite the rage down Poplar way just now."

"It's robbing you," said the mate, "and it's no good either. I ain't got a decent suit of clothes to my back."

Evans looked up, and their eyes met; then, with a catch in his breath, he turned away, and after some hesitation went to his locker, and bringing out a new suit, bought for the edification of Miss Jones, handed it silently to the mate.

"I can't take all these things without giving you something for 'em," said the mate. "Here, wait a bit."

He dived into his cabin, and, after a hasty search, brought out some garments which he placed on the table before his commander.

"I wouldn't wear 'em, no, not to drown myself in," declared Evans after a brief glance; "they ain't even decent."

"So much the better," said the mate; "it'll be more of a contrast with me."

After a slight contest the skipper gave way, and the mate, after an elaborate toilette, went on deck and began to make himself agreeable, while his chief skulked below trying to muster up courage to put in an appearance.

"Where's the captain?" inquired Miss Cooper, after his absence had been so prolonged as to become noticeable.

"He's below, dressin', I b'leeve," replied the mate simply.

Miss Cooper, glancing at his attire, smiled softly to herself, and prepared for something startling, and she got t; for a more forlorn, sulky-looking object than the skipper, when he did appear, had never been seen on the deck of the Falcon, and his London betrothed glanced at him hot with shame and indignation.

"Whatever have you got those things on for?" she whispered.

"Work, my dear—work," replied the skipper.

"Well, mind you don't lose any of the pieces," said the dear suavely; "you mightn't be able to match that cloth."

"I'll look after that," said the skipper, reddening. "You must excuse me talkin' to you now. I'm busy."

Miss Cooper looked at him indignantly, and, biting her lip, turned away, and started a desperate flirtation with the mate, to punish him. Evans watched them with mingled feelings as he busied himself with various small jobs on the deck, his wrath being raised to boiling point by the behaviour of the cook, who, being a poor hand at disguising his feelings, came out of the galley several times to look at him.

From this incident a coolness sprang up between the skipper and the girl, which increased hourly. At times the skipper weakened, but the watchful mate was always on hand to prevent mischief. Owing to his fostering care Evans was generally busy, and always gruff; and Miss Cooper, who was used to the most assiduous attentions from him, knew not whether to be most bewildered or most indignant. Four times in one day did he remark in her hearing that a sailor's ship was his sweetheart, while h s treatment of his small prospective brother in-law, when he expostulated with him on the state of his wardrobe, filled that hitherto pampered youth with amazement. At last, on the fourth night out, as the little schooner was passing the coast of Cornwall, the mate came up to him as he was steering, and patted him heavily on the back.

"It's all right, cap'n," said he. "You've lost the prettiest little girl in England."

"What?" said the skipper, in incredulous tones.

"Fact," replied the other. "Here's your ring back. I wouldn't let her wear it any longer."

"However did you do it?" inquired Evans, taking the ring in a dazed fashion.

"Oh, easy as possible," said the mate. "She liked me best, that's all."

"But what did you say to her?" persisted Evans.

The other reflected.

"I can't call to mind exactly," he said at length. "But, you may rely upon it, I said everything I could against you. But she never did care much for you. She told me so herself."

"I wish you joy of your bargain," said Evans solemnly, after a long pause.

"What do you mean?" demanded the mate sharply.

"A girl like that," said the skipper, with a lump in his throat, "who can carry on with two men at once ain't worth having. She's not my money, that's all."

The mate looked at him in honest bewilderment.

"Mark my words," continued the skipper loftily, "you'll live to regret it. A girl like that's got no ballast. She'll always be running after fresh neckties."

"You put it down to the necktie, do you?" sneered the mate wrathfully.

"That and the clothes, cert'nly," replied the skipper.

"Well, you're wrong," said the mate. "A lot you know about girls. It wasn't your old clothes, and it wasn't all your bad behaviour to her since she's been aboard. You may as well know first as last. She wouldn't have nothing to do with me at first, so I told her all about Mary Jones."

"You told her THAT?" cried the skipper fiercely.

"I did," replied the other. "She was pretty wild at first; but then the comic side of it struck her—you wearing them old clothes, and going about as you did. She used to watch you until she couldn't stand it any longer, and then go down in the cabin and laugh. Wonderful spirits that girl's got. Hush! Here she is!"

As he spoke the girl came on deck, and, seeing the two men talking together, remained at a short distance from them.

"It's all right, Jane," said the mate; "I've told him."

"Oh!" said Miss Cooper, with a little gasp.

"I can't bear deceit," said the mate; "and now it's off his mind, he's so happy he can't bear himself."

The latter part of this assertion seemed to be more warranted by facts than the former, but Evans made a choking noise, which he intended as a sign of unbearable joy, and, relinquishing the wheel to the mate, walked forward. The clear sky was thick with stars, and a mind at ease might have found enjoyment in the quiet beauty of the night, but the skipper was too interested in the behaviour of the young couple at the wheel to give it a thought. Immersed in each other, they forgot him entirely, and exchanged little playful slaps and pushes, which incensed him beyond description. Several times he was on the point of exercising his position as commander and ordering the mate below, but in the circumstances interference was impossible, and, with a low-voiced good-night, he went below. Here his gaze fell on William Henry, who was slumbering peacefully, and, with a hazy idea of the eternal fitness of things, he raised the youth in his arms, and, despite his sleepy protests, deposited him in the mate's bunk. Then, with head and heart both aching, he retired for the night.

There was a little embarrassment next day, but it soon passed off, and the three adult inmates of the cabin got on quite easy terms with each other. The most worried person aft was the boy, who had not been taken into their confidence, and whose face, when his sister sat with the mate's arm around her waist, presented to the skipper a perfect study in emotions.

"I feel quite curious to see this Miss Jones," said Miss Cooper amiably, as they sat at dinner.

"She'll be on the quay, waving her handkerchief to him," said the mate. "We'll be in to-morrow afternoon, and then you'll see her."

As it happened, the mate was a few hours out in his reckoning, for by the time the Falcon's bows were laid for the small harbour it was quite dark, and the little schooner glided in, guided by the two lights which marked the entrance. The quay, seen in the light of a few scattered lamps, looked dreary enough, and, except for two or three indistinct figures, appeared to be deserted. Beyond, the broken lights of the town stood out more clearly as the schooner crept slowly over the dark water towards her berth.

"Fine night, cap'n," said the watchman, as the schooner came gently alongside the quay.

The skipper grunted assent. He was peering anxiously at the quay.

"It's too late," said the mate. "You couldn't expect her this time o'night. It's ten o'clock."

"I'll go over in the morning," said Evans, who, now that things had been adjusted, was secretly disappointed that Miss Cooper had not witnessed the meeting. "If you're not going ashore, we might have a hand o' cards as soon's we're made fast."

The mate assenting, they went below, and were soon deep in the mysteries of three-hand cribbage. Evans, who was a good player, surpassed himself, and had just won the first game, the others being nowhere, when a head was thrust down the companion-way, and a voice like a strained foghorn called the captain by name.

"Ay, ay!" yelled Evans, laying down his hand.

"I'll come down, cap'n," said the voice, and the mate just had time to whisper "Old Jones" to Miss Cooper, when a man of mighty bulk filled up the doorway of the little cabin, and extended a huge paw to Evans and the mate. He then looked at the lady, and, breathing hard, waited.

"Young lady o' the mate's," said Evans breathlessly, "Miss Cooper. Sit down, cap'n. Get the gin out, Bill."

"Not for me," said Captain Jones firmly, but with an obvious effort.

The surprise of Evans and the mate admitted of no concealment; but it passed unnoticed by their visitor, who, fidgeting in his seat, appeared to be labouring with some mysterious problem. After a long pause, during which all watched him anxiously, he reached over the table and shook hands with Evans again.

"Put it there, cap'n," said Evans, much affected by this token of esteem.

The old man rose and stood looking at him, with his hand on his shoulder; he then shook hands for the third time, and patted him encouragingly on the back.

"Is anything the matter?" demanded the skipper of the Falcon as he rose to his feet, alarmed by these manifestations of feeling." Is Mary—is she ill?"

"Worse than that," said the other—"worse'n that, my poor boy; she's married a lobster!"

The effect of this communication upon Evans was tremendous; but it may be doubted whether he was more surprised than Miss Cooper, who, utterly unversed in military terms, strove in vain to realize the possibility of such a mesalliance, as she gazed wildly at the speaker and squeaked with astonishment.

"When was it?" asked Evans at last, in a dull voice.

"Thursday fortnight, at ha' past eleven," said the old man. "He's a sergeant in the line. I would have written to you, but I thought it was best to come and break it to you gently. Cheer up, my boy; there's more than one Mary Jones in the world."

With this undeniable fact, Captain Jones waved a farewell to the party and went off, leaving them to digest his news. For some time they sat still, the mate and Miss Cooper exchanging whispers, until at length, the stillness becoming oppressive, they withdrew to their respective berths, leaving the skipper sitting at the table, gazing hard at a knot in the opposite locker.

For long after their departure he sat thus, amid a deep silence, broken only by an occasional giggle from the stateroom, or an idiotic sniggering from the direction of the mate's bunk, until, recalled to mundane affairs by the lamp burning itself out, he went, in befitting gloom, to bed.

"MATRIMONIAL OPENINGS"

Mr. Dowson sat by the kitchen fire smoking and turning a docile and well-trained ear to the heated words which fell from his wife's lips.

"She'll go and do the same as her sister Jenny done," said Mrs. Dowson, with a side glance at her daughter Flora; "marry a man and then 'ave to work and slave herself to skin and bone to keep him."

"I see Jenny yesterday," said her husband, nodding. "Getting quite fat, she is."

"That's right," said Mrs. Dowson, violently, "that's right! The moment I say something you go and try and upset it."

"Un'ealthy fat, p'r'aps," said Mr. Dowson, hurriedly; "don't get enough exercise, I s'pose."

"Anybody who didn't know you, Joe Dowson," said his wife, fiercely, "would think you was doing it a purpose."

"Doing wot?" inquired Mr. Dowson, removing his pipe and regarding her open-mouthed. "I only said—"

"I know what you said," retorted his wife. "Here I do my best from morning to night to make everybody 'appy and comfortable; and what happens?"

"Nothing," said the sympathetic Mr. Dowson, shaking his head. "Nothing."

"Anyway, Jenny ain't married a fool," said Mrs. Dowson, hotly; "she's got that consolation."

"That's right, mother," said the innocent Mr. Dowson, "look on the bright side o' things a bit. If Jenny 'ad married a better chap I don't suppose we should see half as much of her as wot we do."

"I'm talking of Flora," said his wife, restraining herself by an effort. "One unfortunate marriage in the family is enough; and here, instead o' walking out with young Ben Lippet, who'll be 'is own master when his father dies, she's gadding about with that good-for-nothing Charlie Foss."

Mr. Dowson shook his head. "He's so good-looking, is Charlie," he said, slowly; "that's the worst of it. Wot with 'is dark eyes and his curly 'air—"

"Go on!" said his wife, passionately, "go on!"

Mr. Dowson, dimly conscious that something was wrong, stopped and puffed hard at his pipe. Through the cover of the smoke he bestowed a sympathetic wink upon his daughter.

"You needn't go on too fast," said the latter, turning to her mother. "I haven't made up my mind yet. Charlie's looks are all right, but he ain't over and above steady, and Ben is steady, but he ain't much to look at."

"What does your 'art say?" inquired the sentimental Mr. Dowson.

Neither lady took the slightest notice.

"Charlie Foss is too larky," said Mrs. Dowson, solemnly; "it's easy come and easy go with 'im. He's just such another as your father's cousin Bill—and look what 'appened to him!"

Miss Dowson shrugged her shoulders and subsiding in her chair, went on with her book, until a loud knock at the door and a cheerful, but peculiarly shrill, whistle sounded outside.

"There is my lord," exclaimed Mrs. Dowson, waspishly; "anybody might think the 'ouse belonged to him. And now he's dancing on my clean doorstep."

"Might be only knocking the mud off afore coming in," said Mr. Dowson, as he rose to open the door. "I've noticed he's very careful."

"I just came in to tell you a joke," said Mr. Foss, as he followed his host into the kitchen and gazed tenderly at Miss Dowson—"best joke I ever had in my life; I've 'ad my fortune told—guess what it was! I've been laughing to myself ever since."

"Who told it?" inquired Mrs. Dowson, after a somewhat awkward silence.

"Old gypsy woman in Peter Street," replied Mr. Foss. "I gave 'er a wrong name and address, just in case she might ha' heard about me, and she did make a mess of it; upon my word she did."

"Wot did she say?" inquired Mr. Dowson.

Mr. Foss laughed. "Said I was a wrong 'un," he said, cheerfully, "and would bring my mother's gray hairs to the grave with sorrow. I'm to 'ave bad companions and take to drink; I'm to steal money to gamble with, and after all that I'm to 'ave five years for bigamy. I told her I was disappointed I wasn't to be hung, and she said it would be a disappointment to a lot of other people too. Laugh! I thought I should 'ave killed myself."

"I don't see nothing to laugh at," said Mrs. Dowson, coldly.

"I shouldn't tell anybody else, Charlie," said her husband. "Keep it a secret, my boy."

"But you—you don't believe it?" stammered the crestfallen Mr. Foss.

Mrs. Dowson cast a stealthy glance at her daughter. "Its wonderful 'ow some o' those fortune-tellers can see into the future," she said, shaking her head.

"Ah!" said her husband, with a confirmatory nod. "Wonderful is no name for it. I 'ad my fortune told once when I was a boy, and she told me I should marry the prettiest, and the nicest, and the sweetest-tempered gal in Poplar."

Mr. Foss, with a triumphant smile, barely waited for him to finish. "There you—" he began, and stopped suddenly.

"What was you about to remark?" inquired Mrs. Dowson, icily.

"I was going to say," replied Mr. Foss—"I was going to say—I 'ad just got it on the tip o' my tongue to say, 'There you—you—you 'ad all the luck, Mr. Dowson.'"

He edged his chair a little nearer to Flora; but there was a chilliness in the atmosphere against which his high spirits strove in vain. Mr. Dowson remembered other predictions which had come true, notably the case of one man who, learning that he was to come in for a legacy, gave up a two-pound-a-week job, and did actually come in for twenty pounds and a bird-cage seven years afterwards.

"It's all nonsense," protested Mr. Foss; "she only said all that because I made fun of her. You don't believe it, do you, Flora?"

"I don't see anything to laugh at," returned Miss Dowson. "Fancy five years for bigamy! Fancy the disgrace of it!"

"But you're talking as if I was going to do it," objected Mr. Foss. "I wish you'd go and 'ave your fortune told. Go and see what she says about you. P'r'aps you won't believe so much in fortune-telling afterwards."

Mrs. Dowson looked up quickly, and then, lowering her eyes, took her hand out of the stocking she had been darning and, placing it beside its companion, rolled the pair into a ball.

"You go round to-morrow night, Flora," she said, deliberately. "It sha'n't be said a daughter of mine was afraid to hear the truth about herself; father'll find the money."

"And she can say what she likes about you, but I sha'n't believe it," said Mr. Foss, reproachfully.

"I don't suppose it'll be anything to be ashamed of," said Miss Dowson, sharply.

Mr. Foss bade them good-night suddenly, and, finding himself accompanied to the door by Mr. Dowson, gave way to gloom. He stood for so long with one foot on the step and the other on the mat that Mr. Dowson, who disliked draughts, got impatient.

"You'll catch cold, Charlie," he said at last.

"That's what I'm trying to do," said Mr. Foss; "my death o' cold. Then I sha'n't get five years for bigamy," he added bitterly.

"Cheer up," said Mr. Dowson; "five years ain't much out of a lifetime; and you can't expect to 'ave your fun without—"

He watched the retreating figure of Mr. Foss as it stamped its way down the street, and closing the door returned to the kitchen to discuss palmistry and other sciences until bedtime.

Mrs. Dowson saw husband and daughter off to work in the morning, and after washing up the breakfast things drew her chair up to the kitchen fire and became absorbed in memories of the past. All the leading incidents in Flora's career passed in review before her. Measles, whooping-cough, school-prizes, and other things peculiar to the age of innocence were all there. In her enthusiasm she nearly gave her a sprained ankle which had belonged to her sister. Still shaking her head over her mistake, she drew Flora's latest portrait carefully from its place in the album, and putting on her hat and jacket went round to make a call in Peter Street.

By the time Flora returned home Mrs. Dowson appeared to have forgotten the arrangement made the night before, and, being reminded by her daughter, questioned whether any good could come of attempts to peer into the future. Mr. Dowson was still more emphatic, but his objections, being recognized by both ladies as trouser-pocket ones, carried no weight. It ended in Flora going off with half a crown in her glove and an urgent request from her father to make it as difficult as possible for the sibyl by giving a false name and address.

No name was asked for, however, as Miss Dowson was shown into the untidy little back room on the first floor, in which the sorceress ate, slept, and received visitors. She rose from an old rocking-chair as the visitor entered, and, regarding her with a pair of beady black eyes, bade her sit down.

"Are you the fortune-teller?" inquired the girl.

"Men call me so," was the reply.

"Yes, but are you?" persisted Miss Dowson, who inherited her father's fondness for half crowns.

"Yes," said the other, in a more natural voice.

She took the girl's left hand, and pouring a little dark liquid into the palm gazed at it intently. "Left for the past; right for the future," she said, in a deep voice.

She muttered some strange words and bent her head lower over the girl's hand.

"I see a fair-haired infant," she said, slowly; "I see a little girl of four racked with the whooping-cough; I see her later, eight she appears to be. She is in bed with measles."

Miss Dowson stared at her open-mouthed.

"She goes away to the seaside to get strong," continued the sorceress; "she is paddling; she falls into the water and spoils her frock; her mother—"

"Never mind about that," interrupted the staring Miss Dowson, hastily. "I was only eight at the time and mother always was ready with her hands."

"People on the beach smile," resumed the other. "They

"It don't take much to make some people laugh," said Miss Dowson, with bitterness.

"At fourteen she and a boy next door but seven both have the mumps."

"And why not?" demanded Miss Dowson with great warmth. "Why not?"

"I'm only reading what I see in your hand," said the other. "At fifteen I see her knocked down by a boat-swing; a boy from opposite brings her home."

"Passing at the time," murmured Miss Dowson.

"His head is done up with sticking-plaster. I see her apprenticed to a dressmaker. I see her—"

The voice went on monotonously, and Flora, gasping with astonishment, listened to a long recital of the remaining interesting points in her career.

"That brings us to the present," said the soothsayer, dropping her hand. "Now for the future."

She took the girl's other hand and poured some of the liquid into it. Miss Dowson shrank back.

"If it's anything dreadful," she said, quickly, "I don't want to hear it. It—it ain't natural."

"I can warn you of dangers to keep clear of," said the other, detaining her hand. "I can let you peep into the future and see what to do and what to avoid. Ah!"

She bent over the girl's hand again and uttered little ejaculations of surprise and perplexity.

"I see you moving in gay scenes surrounded by happy faces," she said, slowly. "You are much sought after. Handsome presents and fine clothes are showered upon you. You will cross the sea. I see a dark young man and a fair young man. They will both influence your life. The fair young man works in his father's shop. He will have great riches."

"What about the other?" inquired Miss Dowson, after a somewhat lengthy pause.

The fortune-teller shook her head. "He is his own worst enemy," she said, "and he will drag down those he loves with him. You are going to marry one of them, but I can't see clear—I can't see which."

"Look again," said the trembling Flora.

"I can't see," was the reply, "therefore it isn't meant for me to see. It's for you to choose. I can see them now as plain as I can see you. You are all three standing where two roads meet. The fair young man is beckoning to you and pointing to a big house and a motor-car and a yacht."

"And the other?" said the surprised Miss Dowson.

"He's in knickerbockers," said the other, doubtfully. "What does that mean? Ah, I see! They've got the broad arrow on them, and he is pointing to a jail. It's all gone—I can see no more."

She dropped the girl's hand and, drawing her hand across her eyes, sank back into her chair. Miss Dowson, with trembling fingers, dropped the half crown into her lap, and, with her head in a whirl, made her way downstairs.

After such marvels the streets seemed oddly commonplace as she walked swiftly home. She decided as she went to keep her knowledge to herself, but inclination on the one hand and Mrs. Dowson on the other got the better of her resolution. With the exception of a few things in her past, already known and therefore not worth dwelling upon, the whole of the interview was disclosed.

"It fair takes your breath away," declared the astounded Mr. Dowson.

"The fair young man is meant for Ben Lippet," said his wife, "and the dark one is Charlie Foss. It must be. It's no use shutting your eyes to things."

"It's as plain as a pikestaff," agreed her husband. "And she told Charlie five years for bigamy, and when she's telling Flora's Fortune she sees 'im in convict's clothes. How she does it I can't think."

"It's a gift," said Mrs. Dowson, briefly, "and I do hope that Flora is going to act sensible. Anyhow, she can let Ben Lippet come and see her, without going upstairs with the tooth-ache."

"He can come if he likes," said Flora; "though why Charlie couldn't have 'ad the motor-car and 'im the five years, I don't know."

Mr. Lippet came in the next evening, and the evening after. In fact, so easy is it to fall into habits of an agreeable nature that nearly every evening saw him the happy guest of Mr. Dowson. A spirit of resignation, fostered by a present or two and a visit to the theatre, descended upon Miss Dowson. Fate and her mother combined were in a fair way to overcome her inclinations, when Mr. Foss, who had been out of town on a job, came in to hear the result of her visit to the fortune-teller, and found Mr. Lippet installed in the seat that used to be his.

At first Mrs. Dowson turned a deaf ear to his request for information, and it was only when his jocularity on the subject passed the bounds of endurance that she consented to gratify his curiosity.

"I didn't want to tell you," she said, when she had finished, "but you asked for it, and now you've got it."

"It's very amusing," said Mr. Foss. "I wonder who the dark young man in the fancy knickers is?"

"Ah, I daresay you'll know some day," said Mrs. Dowson.

"Was the fair young man a good-looking chap?" inquired the inquisitive Mr. Foss.

Mrs. Dowson hesitated. "Yes," she said, defiantly.

"Wonder who it can be?" muttered Mr. Foss, in perplexity.

"You'll know that too some day, no doubt," was the reply.

"I'm glad it's to be a good-looking chap," he said; "not that I think Flora believes in such rubbish as fortune-telling. She's too sensible."

"I do," said Flora. "How should she know all the things I did when I was a little girl? Tell me that."

"I believe in it, too," said Mrs. Dowson. "P'r'aps you'll tell me I'm not sensible!"

Mr. Foss quailed at the challenge and relapsed into moody silence. The talk turned on an aunt of Mr. Lippet's, rumored to possess money, and an uncle who was "rolling" in it. He began to feel in the way, and only his native obstinacy prevented him from going.

It was a relief to him when the front door opened and the heavy step of Mr. Dowson was heard in the tiny passage. If anything it seemed heavier than usual, and Mr. Dowson's manner when he entered the room and greeted his guests was singularly lacking in its usual cheerfulness. He drew a chair to the fire, and putting his feet on the fender gazed moodily between the bars.

"I've been wondering as I came along," he said at last, with an obvious attempt to speak carelessly, "whether this 'ere fortune-telling as we've been hearing so much about lately always comes out true."

"It depends on the fortune-teller," said his wife.

"I mean," said Mr. Dowson, slowly, "I mean that gypsy woman that Charlie and Flora went to."

"Of course it does," snapped his wife. "I'd trust what she says afore anything."

"I know five or six that she has told," said Mr. Lippet, plucking up courage; "and they all believe 'er. They couldn't help themselves; they said so."

"Still, she might make a mistake sometimes," said Mr. Dowson, faintly. "Might get mixed up, so to speak."

"Never!" said Mrs. Dowson, firmly.

"Never!" echoed Flora and Mr. Lippet.

Mr. Dowson heaved a big sigh, and his eye wandered round the room. It lighted on Mr. Foss.

"She's an old humbug," said that gentleman. "I've a good mind to put the police on to her."

Mr. Dowson reached over and gripped his hand. Then he sighed again.

"Of course, it suits Charlie Foss to say so," said Mrs. Dowson; "naturally he'd say so; he's got reasons. I believe every word she says. If she told me I was coming in for a fortune I should believe her; and if she told me I was going to have misfortunes I should believe her."

"Don't say that," shouted Mr. Dowson, with startling energy. "Don't say that. That's what she did say!"

"What?" cried his wife, sharply. "What are you talking about?"

"I won eighteenpence off of Bob Stevens," said her husband, staring at the table. "Eighteenpence is 'er price for telling the future only, and, being curious and feeling I'd like to know what's going to 'appen to me, I went in and had eighteenpennorth."

"Well, you're upset," said Mrs. Dowson, with a quick glance at him. "You get upstairs to bed."

"I'd sooner stay 'ere," said her husband, resuming his seat; "it seems more cheerful and lifelike. I wish I 'adn't gorn, that's what I wish."

"What did she tell you?" inquired Mr. Foss.

Mr. Dowson thrust his hands into his trouser pockets and spoke desperately. "She says I'm to live to ninety, and I'm to travel to foreign parts—"

"You get to bed," said his wife. "Come along."

Mr. Dowson shook his head doggedly. "I'm to be rich," he continued, slowly—"rich and loved. After my pore dear wife's death I'm to marry again; a young woman with money and stormy brown eyes."

Mrs. Dowson sprang from her chair and stood over him quivering with passion. "How dare you?" she gasped. "You—you've been drinking."

"I've 'ad two arf-pints," said her husband, solemnly. "I shouldn't 'ave 'ad the second only I felt so miserable. I know I sha'n't be 'appy with a young woman."

Mrs. Dowson, past speech, sank back in her chair and stared at him.

"I shouldn't worry about it if I was you, Mrs. Dowson," said Mr. Foss, kindly. "Look what she said about me. That ought to show you she ain't to be relied on."

"Eyes like lamps," said Mr. Dowson, musingly, "and I'm forty-nine next month. Well, they do say every eye 'as its own idea of beauty."

A strange sound, half laugh and half cry, broke from the lips of the over-wrought Mrs. Dowson. She controlled herself by an effort.

"If she said it," she said, doggedly, with a fierce glance at Mr. Foss, "it'll come true. If, after my death, my 'usband is going to marry a young woman with—with—"

"Stormy brown eyes," interjected Mr. Foss, softly.

"It's his fate and it can't be avoided," concluded Mrs. Dowson.

"But it's so soon," said the unfortunate husband. "You're to die in three weeks and I'm to be married three months after."

Mrs. Dowson moistened her lips and tried, but in vain, to avoid the glittering eye of Mr. Foss. "Three!" she said, mechanically, "three! three weeks!"

"Don't be frightened," said Mr. Foss, in a winning voice. "I don't believe it; and, besides, we shall soon see! And if you don't die in three weeks, perhaps I sha'n't get five years for bigamy, and perhaps Flora won't marry a fair man with millions of money and motor-cars."

"No; perhaps she is wrong after all, mother," said Mr. Dowson, hopefully.

Mrs. Dowson gave him a singularly unkind look for one about to leave him so soon, and, afraid to trust herself to speech, left the room and went up-stairs. As the door closed behind her, Mr. Foss took the chair which Mr. Lippet had thoughtlessly vacated, and offered such consolations to Flora as he considered suitable to the occasion.

MIXED RELATIONS

The brig Elizabeth Barstow came up the river as though in a hurry to taste again the joys of the Metropolis. The skipper, leaning on the wheel, was in the midst of a hot discussion with the mate, who was placing before him the hygienic, economical, and moral advantages of total abstinence in language of great strength but little variety.

"Teetotallers eat more," said the skipper, finally.

The mate choked, and his eye sought the galley. "Eat more?" he spluttered. "Yesterday the meat was like brick-bats; to-day it tasted like a bit o' dirty sponge. I've lived on biscuits this trip; and the only tater I ate I'm going to see a doctor about direckly I get ashore. It's a sin and a shame to spoil good food the way 'e does."

"The moment I can ship another cook he goes," said the skipper. "He seems busy, judging by the noise."

"I'm making him clean up everything, ready for the next," explained the mate, grimly. "And he 'ad the cheek to tell me he's improving—improving!"

"He'll go as soon as I get another," repeated the skipper, stooping and peering ahead. "I don't like being poisoned any more than you do. He told me he could cook when I shipped him; said his sister had taught him."

The mate grunted and, walking away, relieved his mind by putting his head in at the galley and bidding the cook hold up each separate utensil for his inspection. A hole in the frying-pan the cook modestly attributed to elbow-grease.

The river narrowed, and the brig, picking her way daintily through the traffic, sought her old berth at Buller's Wharf. It was occupied by a deaf sailing-barge, which, moved at last by self-interest, not unconnected with its paint, took up a less desirable position and consoled itself with adjectives.

The men on the wharf had gone for the day, and the crew of the Elizabeth Barstow, after making fast, went below to prepare themselves for an evening ashore. Standing before the largest saucepan-lid in the galley, the cook was putting the finishing touches to his toilet.

A light, quick step on the wharf attracted the attention of the skipper as he leaned against the side smoking. It stopped just behind him, and turning round he found himself gazing into the soft brown eyes of the prettiest girl he had ever seen.

"Is Mr. Jewell on board, please?" she asked, with a smile.

"Jewell?" repeated the skipper. "Jewell? Don't know the name."

"He was on board," said the girl, somewhat taken aback. "This is the Elizabeth Barstow, isn't it?"

"What's his Christian name?" inquired the skipper, thoughtfully.

"Albert," replied the girl. "Bert," she added, as the other shook his head.

"Oh, the cook!" said the skipper. "I didn't know his name was Jewell. Yes, he's in the galley."

He stood eyeing her and wondering in a dazed fashion what she could see in a small, white-faced, slab-sided—

The girl broke in upon his meditations. "How does he cook?" she inquired, smiling.

He was about to tell her, when he suddenly remembered the cook's statement as to his instructor.

"He's getting on," he said, slowly; "he's getting on. Are you his sister?"

The girl smiled and nodded. "Ye—es," she said, slowly. "Will you tell him I am waiting for him, please?"

The skipper started and drew himself up; then he walked forward and put his head in at the galley.

"Bert," he said, in a friendly voice, "your sister wants to see you."

"Who?" inquired Mr. Jewell, in the accents of amazement. He put his head out at the door and nodded, and then, somewhat red in the face with the exercise, drew on his jacket and walked towards her. The skipper followed.

"Thank you," said the girl, with a pleasant smile.

"You're quite welcome," said the skipper.

Mr. Jewell stepped ashore and, after a moment of indecision, shook hands with his visitor.

"If you're down this way again," said the skipper, as they turned away, "perhaps you'd like to see the cabin. We're in rather a pickle just now, but if you should happen to come down for Bert to-morrow night—"

The girl's eyes grew mirthful and her lips trembled. "Thank you," she said.

"Some people like looking over cabins," murmured the skipper.

He raised his hand to his cap and turned away. The mate, who had just come on deck, stared after the retreating couple and gave vent to a low whistle.

"What a fine gal to pick up with Slushy," he remarked.

"It's his sister," said the skipper, somewhat sharply.

"The one that taught him to cook?" said the other, hastily. "Here! I'd like five minutes alone with her; I'd give 'er a piece o' my mind that 'ud do her good. I'd learn 'er. I'd tell 'er wot I thought of her."

"That'll do," said the skipper; "that'll do. He's not so bad for a beginner; I've known worse."

"Not so bad?" repeated the mate. "Not so bad? Why"—his voice trembled— "ain't you going to give 'im the chuck, then?"

"I shall try him for another vy'ge, George," said the skipper. "It's hard lines on a youngster if he don't have a chance. I was never one to be severe. Live and let live, that's my motto. Do as you'd be done by."

"You're turning soft-'arted in your old age," grumbled the mate.

"Old age!" said the other, in a startled voice. "Old age! I'm not thirty-seven yet."

"You're getting on," said the mate; "besides, you look old."

The skipper investigated the charge in the cabin looking-glass ten minutes later. He twisted his beard in his hand and tried to imagine how he would look without it. As a compromise he went out and had it cut short and trimmed to a point. The glass smiled approval on his return; the mate smiled too, and, being caught in the act, said it made him look like his own grandson.

It was late when the cook returned, but the skipper was on deck, and, stopping him for a match, entered into a little conversation. Mr. Jewell, surprised at first, soon became at his ease, and, the talk drifting in some unknown fashion to Miss Jewell, discussed her with brotherly frankness.

"You spent the evening together, I s'pose?" said the skipper, carelessly.

Mr. Jewell glanced at him from the corner of his eye. "Cooking," he said, and put his hand over his mouth with some suddenness.

By the time they parted the skipper had his hand in a friendly fashion on the cook's shoulder, and was displaying an interest in his welfare as unusual as it was gratifying. So unaccustomed was Mr. Jewell to such consideration that he was fain to pause for a moment or two to regain control of his features before plunging into the lamp-lit fo'c'sle.

The mate made but a poor breakfast next morning, but his superior, who saw the hand of Miss Jewell in the muddy coffee and the cremated bacon, ate his with relish. He was looking forward to the evening, the cook having assured him that his sister had accepted his invitation to inspect the cabin, and indeed had talked of little else. The boy was set to work house-cleaning, and, having gleaned a few particulars, cursed the sex with painstaking thoroughness.

It seemed to the skipper a favorable omen that Miss Jewell descended the companion-ladder as though to the manner born; and her exclamations of delight at the cabin completed his satisfaction. The cook, who had followed them below with some trepidation, became reassured, and seating himself on a locker joined modestly in the conversation.

"It's like a doll's-house," declared the girl, as she finished by examining the space-saving devices in the state-room. "Well, I mustn't take up any more of your time."

"I've got nothing to do," said the skipper, hastily. "I—I was thinking of going for a walk; but it's lonely walking about by yourself."

Miss Jewell agreed. She lowered her eyes and looked under the lashes at the skipper.

"I never had a sister," continued the latter, in melancholy accents.

"I don't suppose you would want to take her out if you had," said the girl.

The skipper protested. "Bert takes you out," he said.

"He isn't like most brothers," said Miss Jewell, shifting along the locker and placing her hand affectionately on the cook's shoulder.

"If I had a sister," continued the skipper, in a somewhat uneven voice, "I should take her out. This evening, for instance, I should take her to a theatre."

Miss Jewell turned upon him the innocent face of a child. "It would be nice to be your sister," she said, calmly.

The skipper attempted to speak, but his voice failed him. "Well, pretend you are my sister," he said, at last, "and we'll go to one."

"Pretend?" said Miss Jewell, as she turned and eyed the cook. "Bert wouldn't like that," she said, decidedly.

"N—no," said the cook, nervously, avoiding the skipper's eye.

"It wouldn't be proper," said Miss Jewell, sitting upright and looking very proper indeed.

"I—I meant Bert to come, too," said the skipper; "of course," he added.

The severity of Miss Jewell's expression relaxed. She stole an amused glance at the cook and, reading her instructions in his eye, began to temporize. Ten minutes later the crew of the Elizabeth Barstow in various attitudes of astonishment beheld their commander going ashore with his cook. The mate so far forgot himself as to whistle, but with great presence of mind cuffed the boy's ear as the skipper turned.

For some little distance the three walked along in silence. The skipper was building castles in the air, the cook was not quite at his ease, and the girl, gazing steadily in front of her, appeared slightly embarrassed.

By the time they reached Aldgate and stood waiting for an omnibus Miss Jewell found herself assailed by doubts. She remembered that she did not want to go to a theatre, and warmly pressed the two men to go together and leave her to go home. The skipper remonstrated in vain, but the cook came to the rescue, and Miss Jewell, still protesting, was pushed on to a 'bus and propelled upstairs. She took a vacant seat in front, and the skipper and Mr. Jewell shared one behind.

The three hours at the theatre passed all too soon, although the girl was so interested in the performance that she paid but slight attention to her companions. During the waits she became interested in her surroundings, and several times called the skipper's attention to smart-looking men in the stalls and boxes. At one man she stared so persistently that an opera-glass was at last levelled in return.

"How rude of him," she said, smiling sweetly at the skipper.

She shook her head in disapproval, but the next moment he saw her gazing steadily at the opera-glasses again.

"If you don't look he'll soon get tired of it," he said, between his teeth.

"Yes, perhaps he will," said Miss Jewell, without lowering her eyes in the least.

The skipper sat in torment until the lights were lowered and the curtain went up again. When it fell he began to discuss the play, but Miss Jewell returned such vague replies that it was evident her thoughts were far away.

"I wonder who he is?" she whispered, gazing meditatingly at the box.

"A waiter, I should think," snapped the skipper.

The girl shook her head. "No, he is much too distinguished-looking," she said, seriously. "Well, I suppose he'll know me again."

The skipper felt that he wanted to get up and smash things; beginning with the man in the box. It was his first love episode for nearly ten years, and he had forgotten the pains and penalties which attach to the condition. When the performance was over he darted a threatening glance at the box, and, keeping close to Miss Jewell, looked carefully about him to make sure that they were not followed.

"It was ripping," said the cook, as they emerged into the fresh air.

"Lovely," said the girl, in a voice of gentle melancholy. "I shall come and see it again, perhaps, when you are at sea."

"Not alone?" said the skipper, in a startled voice.

"I don't mind being alone," said Miss Jewell, gently; "I'm used to it."

The other's reply was lost in the rush for the 'bus, and for the second time that evening the skipper had to find fault with the seating arrangements. And when a vacancy by the side of Miss Jewell did occur, he was promptly forestalled by a young man in a check suit smoking a large cigar.

They got off at Aldgate, and the girl thanked him for a pleasant evening. A hesitating offer to see her home was at once negatived, and the skipper, watching her and the cook until they disappeared in the traffic, walked slowly and thoughtfully to his ship.

The brig sailed the next evening at eight o'clock, and it was not until six that the cook remarked, in the most casual manner, that his sister was coming down to see him off. She arrived half an hour late, and, so far from wanting to see the cabin again, discovered an inconvenient love of fresh air. She came down at last, at the instance of the cook, and, once below, her mood changed, and she treated the skipper with a soft graciousness which raised him to the seventh heaven. "You'll be good to Bert, won't you?" she inquired, with a smile at that young man.

"I'll treat him like my own brother," said the skipper, fervently. "No, better than that; I'll treat him like your brother."

The cook sat erect and, the skipper being occupied with Miss Jewell, winked solemnly at the skylight.

"I know you will," said the girl, very softly; "but I don't think the men—"

"The men'll do as I wish," said the skipper, sternly. "I'm the master on this ship—she's half mine, too—and anybody who interferes with him interferes with me. If there's anything you don't like, Bert, you tell me."

Mr. Jewell, his small, black eyes sparkling, promised, and then, muttering something about his work, exchanged glances with the girl and went up on deck.

"It is a nice cabin," said Miss Jewell, shifting an inch and a half nearer to the skipper. "I suppose poor Bert has to have his meals in that stuffy little place at the other end of the ship, doesn't he?"

"The fo'c'sle?" said the skipper, struggling between love and discipline. "Yes."

The girl sighed, and the mate, who was listening at the skylight above, held his breath with anxiety. Miss Jewell sighed again and in an absent-minded fashion increased the distance between herself and companion by six inches.

"It's usual," faltered the skipper.

"Yes, of course," said the girl, coldly.

"But if Bert likes to feed here, he's welcome," said the skipper, desperately, "and he can sleep aft, too. The mate can say what he likes."

The mate rose and, walking forward, raised his clenched fists to heaven and availed himself of the permission to the fullest extent of a somewhat extensive vocabulary.

"Do you know what I think you are?" inquired Miss Jewell, bending towards him with a radiant face.

"No," said the other, trembling. "What?"

The girl paused. "It wouldn't do to tell you," she said, in a low voice. "It might make you vain."

"Do you know what I think you are?" inquired the skipper in his turn.

Miss Jewell eyed him composedly, albeit the corners of her mouth trembled. "Yes," she said, unexpectedly.

Steps sounded above and came heavily down the companion-ladder. "Tide's a'most on the turn," said the mate, gruffly, from the door.

The skipper hesitated, but the mate stood aside for the girl to pass, and he followed her up on deck and assisted her to the jetty. For hours afterwards he debated with himself whether she really had allowed her hand to stay in his a second or two longer than necessary, or whether unconscious muscular action on his part was responsible for the phenomenon.

He became despondent as they left London behind, but the necessity of interfering between a goggle-eyed and obtuse mate and a pallid but no less obstinate cook helped to relieve him.

"He says he is going to sleep aft," choked the mate, pointing to the cook's bedding.

"Quite right," said the skipper. "I told him to. He's going to take his meals here, too. Anything to say against it?"

The mate sat down on a locker and fought for breath. The cook, still pale, felt his small, black mustache and eyed him with triumphant malice. "I told 'im they was your orders," he remarked.

"And I told him I didn't believe him," said the mate. "Nobody would. Whoever 'eard of a cook living aft? Why, they'd laugh at the idea."

He laughed himself, but in a strangely mirthless fashion, and, afraid to trust himself, went up on deck and brooded savagely apart. Nor did he come down to breakfast until the skipper and cook had finished.

Mr. Jewell bore his new honors badly, and the inability to express their dissatisfaction by means of violence had a bad effect on the tempers of the crew. Sarcasm they did try, but at that the cook could more than hold his own, and, although the men doubted his ability at first, he was able to prove to them by actual experiment that he could cook worse than they supposed.

The brig reached her destination—Creekhaven—on the fifth day, and Mr. Jewell found himself an honored guest at the skipper's cottage. It was a comfortable place, but, as the cook pointed out, too large for one. He also referred, incidentally, to his sister's love of a country life, and, finding himself on a subject of which the other never tired, gave full reins to a somewhat picturesque imagination.

They were back at London within the fortnight, and the skipper learned to his dismay that Miss Jewell was absent on a visit. In these circumstances he would have clung to the cook, but that gentleman, pleading engagements, managed to elude him for two nights out of the three.

On the third day Miss Jewell returned to London, and, making her way to the wharf, was just in time to wave farewells as the brig parted from the wharf.

From the fact that the cook was not visible at the moment the skipper took the salutation to himself. It cheered him for the time, but the next day he was so despondent that the cook, by this time thoroughly in his confidence, offered to write when they got to Creekhaven and fix up an evening.

"And there's really no need for you to come, Bert," said the skipper, cheering up.

Mr. Jewell shook his head. "She wouldn't go without me," he said, gravely. "You've no idea 'ow particular she is. Always was from a child."

"Well, we might lose you," said the skipper, reflecting. "How would that be?"

"We might try it," said the cook, without enthusiasm.

To his dismay the skipper, before they reached London again, had invented at least a score of ways by which he might enjoy Miss Jewell's company without the presence of a third person, some of them so ingenious that the cook, despite his utmost efforts, could see no way of opposing them.

The skipper put his ideas into practice as soon as they reached London. Between Wapping and Charing Cross he lost the cook three times. Miss Jewell found him twice, and the third time she was so difficult that the skipper had to join in the treasure-hunt himself. The cook listened unmoved to a highly-colored picture of his carelessness from the lips of Miss Jewell, and bestowed a sympathetic glance upon the skipper as she paused for breath.

"It's as bad as taking a child out," said the latter, with well-affected indignation.

"Worse," said the girl, tightening her lips.

With a perseverance worthy of a better cause the skipper nudged the cook's arm and tried again. This time he was successful beyond his wildest dreams, and, after ten minutes' frantic search, found that he had lost them both. He wandered up and down for hours, and it was past eleven when he returned to the ship and found the cook waiting for him.

"We thought something 'ad happened to you," said the cook. "Kate has been in a fine way about it. Five minutes after you lost me she found me, and we've been hunting 'igh and low ever since."

Miss Jewell expressed her relief the next evening, and, stealing a glance at the face of the skipper, experienced a twinge of something which she took to be remorse. Ignoring the cook's hints as to theatres, she elected to go for a long 'bus ride, and, sitting in front with the skipper, left Mr. Jewell to keep a chaperon's eye on them from three seats behind.

Conversation was for some time disjointed; then the brightness and crowded state of the streets led the skipper to sound his companion as to her avowed taste for a country life.

"I should love it," said Miss Jewell, with a sigh. "But there's no chance of it; I've got my living to earn."

"You might—might marry somebody living in the country," said the skipper, in trembling tones.

Miss Jewell shuddered. "Marry!" she said, scornfully.

"Most people do," said the other.

"Sensible people don't," said the girl. "You haven't," she added, with a smile.

"I'm very thankful I haven't," retorted the skipper, with great meaning.

"There you are!" said the girl, triumphantly.

"I never saw anybody I liked," said the skipper, "be—before."

"If ever I did marry," said Miss Jewell, with remarkable composure, "if ever I was foolish enough to do such a thing, I think I would marry a man a few years younger than myself."

"Younger?" said the dismayed skipper.

Miss Jewell nodded. "They make the best husbands," she said, gravely.

The skipper began to argue the point, and Mr. Jewell, at that moment taking a seat behind, joined in with some heat. A more ardent supporter could not have been found, although his repetition of the phrase "May and December" revealed a want of tact of which the skipper had not thought him capable. What had promised to be a red-letter day in his existence was spoiled, and he went to bed that night with the full conviction that he had better abandon a project so hopeless.

With a fine morning his courage revived, but as voyage succeeded voyage he became more and more perplexed. The devotion of the cook was patent to all men, but Miss Jewell was as changeable as a weather-glass. The skipper would leave her one night convinced that he had better forget her as soon as possible, and the next her manner would be so kind, and her glances so soft, that only the presence of the ever-watchful cook prevented him from proposing on the spot. The end came one evening in October. The skipper had hurried back from the City, laden with stores, Miss Jewell having, after many refusals, consented to grace the tea-table that afternoon. The table, set by the boy, groaned beneath the weight of unusual luxuries, but the girl had not arrived. The cook was also missing, and the only occupant of the cabin was the mate, who, sitting at one corner, was eating with great relish.

"Ain't you going to get your tea?" he inquired.

"No hurry," said the skipper, somewhat incensed at his haste. "It wouldn't have hurt you to have waited a bit."

"Waited?" said the other. "What for?"

"For my visitors," was the reply.

The mate bit a piece off a crust and stirred his tea. "No use waiting for them," he said, with a grin. "They ain't coming."

"What do you mean?" demanded the skipper.

"I mean," said the mate, continuing to stir his tea with great enjoyment—"I mean that all that kind'artedness of yours was clean chucked away on that cook. He's got a berth ashore and he's gone for good. He left you 'is love; he left it with Bill Hemp."

"Berth ashore?" said the skipper, staring.

"Ah!" said the mate, taking a large and noisy sip from his cup. "He's been fooling you all along for what he could get out of you. Sleeping aft and feeding aft, nobody to speak a word to 'im, and going out and being treated by the skipper; Bill said he laughed so much when he was telling 'im that the tears was running down 'is face like rain. He said he'd never been treated so much in his life."

"That'll do," said the skipper, quickly.

"You ought to hear Bill tell it," said the mate, regretfully. "I can't do it anything like as well as what he can. Made us all roar, he did. What amused 'em most was you thinking that that gal was cookie's sister."

The skipper, with a sharp exclamation, leaned forward, staring at him.

"They're going to be married at Christmas," said the mate, choking in his cup.

The skipper sat upright again, and tried manfully to compose his features. Many things he had not understood before were suddenly made clear, and he remembered now the odd way in which the girl had regarded him as she bade him good-night on the previous evening. The mate eyed him with interest, and was about to supply him with further details when his attention was attracted by footsteps descending the companion-ladder. Then he put down his cup with great care, and stared in stolid amazement at the figure of Miss Jewell in the doorway.

"I'm a bit late," she said, flushing slightly.

She crossed over and shook hands with the skipper, and, in the most natural fashion in the world, took a seat and began to remove her gloves. The mate swung round and regarded her open-mouthed; the skipper, whose ideas were in a whirl, sat regarding her in silence. The mate was the first to move; he left the cabin rubbing his shin, and casting furious glances at the skipper.

"You didn't expect to see me?" said the girl, reddening again.

"No," was the reply.

The girl looked at the tablecloth. "I came to beg your pardon," she said, in a low voice.

"There's nothing to beg my pardon for," said the skipper, clearing his throat. "By rights I ought to beg yours. You did quite right to make fun of me. I can see it now."

"When you asked me whether I was Bert's sister I didn't like to say 'no,' continued the girl; "and at first I let you come out with me for the fun of the thing, and then Bert said it would be good for him, and then—then—"

"Yes," said the skipper, after a long pause.

The girl broke a biscuit into small pieces, and arranged them on the cloth. "Then I didn't mind your coming so much," she said, in a low voice.

The skipper caught his breath and tried to gaze at the averted face.

The girl swept the crumbs aside and met his gaze squarely. "Not quite so much," she explained.

"I've been a fool," said the skipper. "I've been a fool. I've made myself a laughing-stock all round, but if I could have it all over again I would."

"That can never be," said the girl, shaking her head. "Bert wouldn't come."

"No, of course not," asserted the other.

The girl bit her lip. The skipper thought that he had never seen her eyes so large and shining. There was a long silence.

"Good-by," said the girl at last, rising.

The skipper rose to follow. "Good-by," he said, slowly; "and I wish you both every happiness."

"Happiness?" echoed the girl, in a surprised voice. "Why?"

"When you are married."

"I am not going to be married," said the girl. "I told Bert so this afternoon. Good-by."

The skipper actually let her get nearly to the top of the ladder before he regained his presence of mind. Then, in obedience to a powerful tug at the hem of her skirt, she came down again, and accompanied him meekly back to the cabin.

MONEY CHANGERS

Tain't no use waiting any longer," said Harry Pilchard, looking over the side of the brig towards the Tower stairs. "'E's either waiting for the money or else 'e's a-spending of it. Who's coming ashore?"

"Give 'im another five minutes, Harry," said another seaman persuasively; "it 'ud be uncommon 'ard on 'im if 'e come aboard and then 'ad to go an' get another ship's crew to 'elp 'im celebrate it."

"'Ard on us too," said the cook honestly. "There he is!"

The other glanced up at a figure waving to them from the stairs. "'E wants the boat," he said, moving aft.

"No 'e don't, Steve," piped the boy. "'E's waving you not to. He's coming in the waterman's skiff."

"Ha! same old tale," said the seaman wisely. "Chap comes in for a bit o' money and begins to waste it directly. There's threepence gone; clean chucked away. Look at 'im. Just look at him!"

"'E's got the money all right," said the cook, "there's no doubt about that. Why, 'e looks 'arf as large again as 'e did this morning."

The crew bent over the side as the skiff approached, and the fare, who had been leaning back in the stern with a severely important air, rose slowly and felt in his trousers-pocket.

"There's sixpence for you, my lad," he said pompously. "Never mind about the change."

"All right, old slack-breeches," said the waterman with effusive good-fellowship: "up you get."

Three pairs of hands assisted the offended fare on board, and the boy hovering round him slapped his legs vigorously.

"Wot are you up to?" demanded Mr. Samuel Dodds, A.B., turning on him.

"Only dusting you down, Sam," said the boy humbly.

"You got the money all right, I s'pose, Sammy?" said Steve Martin.

Mr. Dodds nodded and slapped his breastpocket.

"Right as ninepence," he replied genially. "I've been with my lawyer all the arternoon, pretty near. 'E's a nice feller."

"'Ow much is it, Sam?" inquired Pilchard eagerly.

"One 'undred and seventy-three pun seventeen shillings an' ten pence," said the heir, noticing with much pleasure the effect of his announcement.

"Say it agin, Sam," said Pilchard in awed tones.

Mr. Dodds, with a happy laugh, obliged him. "If you'll all come down the foc'sle," he continued, "I've got a bundle o' cigars an' a drop o' something short in my pocket."

"Let's 'ave a look at the money, Sam," said Pilchard when the cigars were alight.

"Ah, let's 'ave a look at it," said Steve.

Mr. Dodds laughed again, and, producing a small canvas bag from his pocket, dusted the table with his big palm, and spread out a roll of banknotes and a little pile of gold and silver. It was an impressive sight, and the cook breathed so hard that one note fluttered off the table. Three men dived to recover it, while Sam, alive for the first time to the responsibilities of wealth, anxiously watched the remainder of his capital.

"There's something for you to buy sweets with, my lad," he said, restored to good-humour as the note was replaced.

He passed over a small coin, and regarded with tolerant good-humour the extravagant manifestation of joy on the part of the youth which followed. He capered joyously for a minute or two, and than taking it to the foot of the steps, where the light was better, bit it ecstatically.

"How much is it?" inquired the wondering Steve. "You do chuck your money about, Sam."

"On'y sixpence," said Sam, laughing. "I expect if it 'ad been a shillin' it 'ud ha' turned his brain."

"It ain't a sixpence," said the boy indignantly. "It's 'arf a suvrin'."

"'Arf a wot?" exclaimed Mr. Dodds with a sudden change of manner.

"'Arf a suvrin'," repeated the boy with nervous rapidity; "and thank-you very much, Sam, for your generosity. If everybody was like you we should all be the better for it The world 'ud be a different place to live in," concluded the youthful philosopher.

Mr. Dodd's face under these fulsome praises was a study in conflicting emotions. "Well, don't waste it," he said at length, and hastily gathering up the remainder stowed it in the bag.

"What are you going to do with it all, Sam?" inquired Harry.

"I ain't made up my mind yet," said Mr. Dodds deliberately. "I 'ave thought of 'ouse property."

"I don't mean that," said the other. "I mean, wot are you going to do with it now, to take care of it?"

"Why, keep it in my pocket," said Sam, staring.

"Well, if I was you," said Harry impressively, "I should ask the skipper to take care of it for me. You know wot you are when you're a bit on, Sam."

"Wot d' yer mean?" demanded Mr. Dodds hotly.

"I mean," said Harry hastily, "that you've got sich a generous nature that when you've 'ad a glass or two you're just as likely as not to give it away to somebody."

"I know what I'm about," said Mr. Dodds with conviction. "I'm not goin' to get on while I've got this about me. I'm just goin' round to the 'Bull's Head,' but I shan't drink anything to speak of myself. Anybody that likes to come t'ave anything at my expense is welcome."

A flattering murmur, which was music to Mr. Dodds' ear, arose from his shipmates as they went on deck and hauled the boat alongside. The boy was first in her, and pulling out his pocket-handkerchief ostentatiously wiped down a seat for Mr. Dodds.

"Understand," said that gentleman, with whom the affair of the half-sovereign still rankled, "your drink is shandygaff."

They returned to the brig at eleven o'clock, Mr. Dodds slumbering peacefully in the stern of the boat, propped up on either side by Steve and the boy.

His sleep was so profound that he declined to be aroused, and was hoisted over the side with infinite difficulty and no little risk by his shipmates.

"Look at 'im," said Harry, as they lowered him down the forecastle. "What 'ud ha' become of 'im if we hadn't been with 'im? Where would 'is money ha' been?"

"He'll lose it as sure as eggs is heggs," said Steve, regarding him intently. "Bear a hand to lift 'im in his bunk, Harry."

Harry complied, their task being rendered somewhat difficult by a slight return of consciousness in Mr. Dodds' lower limbs, which, spreading themselves out fan wise, defied all attempts to pack them in the bunk.

"Let 'em hang out then," said Harry savagely, wiping a little mud from his face. "Fancy that coming in for a fortin."

"'E won't 'ave it long," said the cook, shaking his head.

"Wot 'e wants is a shock," said Harry. "'Ow'd it be when he wakes up to tell 'im he's lost all 'is money?"

"Wot's the good o' telling 'im," demanded the cook, "when 'e's got it in his pocket?"

"Well, let's take it out," said Pilchard. "I'll hide it under my piller, and let him think he's 'ad his pocket picked."

"I won't 'ave nothing to do with it," said Steve peremptorily. "I don't believe in sich games."

"Wot do you think, cook?" inquired Harry.

"I don't see no 'arm in it," said the cook slowly; "the fright might do 'im good, p'raps."

"It might be the saving of 'im," said Harry. He leaned over the sleeping seaman, and, gently inserting his fingers in his breast-pocket, drew out the canvas bag. "There it is, chaps," he said gaily; "an' I'll give 'im sich a fright in the morning as he won't forget in a 'urry."

He retired to his bunk, and placing the bag under his pillow, was soon fast asleep. The other men followed his example, and Steve extinguishing the lamp, the forecastle surrendered itself to sleep.

At five o'clock they were awakened by the voice of Mr. Dodds. It was a broken, disconnected sort of voice at first, like to that of a man talking in his sleep; but as Mr. Dodds' head cleared his ideas cleared with it, and in strong, forcible language straight from the heart he consigned the eyes and limbs of some person or persons unknown to every variety of torment; after which, in a voice broken with emotion, he addressed himself in terms of heartbreaking sympathy.

"Shut up, Sam," said Harry in a sleepy voice. "Why can't you go to sleep?"

"Sleep be 'anged," said Mr. Dodds tearfully. "I've lorst all my money."

"You're dreamin'," said Harry lightly; "pinch yourself."

Mr. Dodds, who had a little breath left and a few words still comparatively fresh, bestowed them upon him.

"I tell you you haven't lorst it," said Harry. "Don't you remember giving it to that red-'aired woman with a baby?"

"Wot?" said the astounded Mr. Dodds.

"You give it to 'er an' told 'er to buy the baby a bun with it," continued the veracious Mr. Pilchard.

"Told 'er to buy the baby a bun with it?" repeated Mr. Dodds in a dazed voice. "Told 'er to—Wot did you let me do it for? Wot was all you chaps standin' by an' doin' to let me go an' do it for?"

"We did arsk you not to," said Steve, joining in the conversation.

Mr. Dodds finding language utterly useless to express his burning thoughts, sat down and madly smashed at the table with his fists.

"Wot was you a-doin' to let me do it?" he demanded at length of the boy. "You ungrateful little toad. You can give me that 'arf-suvrin back, d'ye hear?"

"I can't," said the boy. "I followed your example, and give it to the red-'aired woman to buy the baby another bun with."

There was a buzzing noise in Mr. Dodds' head, and the bunks and their grinning occupants went round and round.

"'Ere, 'old up, Sam," said Pilchard, shaking him in alarm. "It's all right; don't be a fool. I've got the money."

Sam stared at him blankly.

"I've got the money," repeated the seaman.

Mr. Dodds' colour came back.

"How'd you get it?" he inquired.

"I took it out of your pocket last night just to give you a lesson," said Harry severely. "Don't you never be so silly agin, Sam."

"Gimme my money," said Mr. Dodds, glaring at him.

"You might ha' lorst it, you see, Sam," continued his benefactor; "if I could take it, anybody else could. Let this be a lesson to you."

"If you don't grimme my money—" began Sam violently.

"It's no good trying to do 'im a kindness," said Harry to the others as he turned to his bunk. "He can go an' lose it for all I care."

He put his hand in his bunk, and then with a sudden exclamation searched somewhat hastily amongst the bedding. Mr. Dodds, watching him with a scowl, saw him take every article separately out of his bunk, and then sink down appalled on the locker.

"You've took it, Sam—ain't—you?" he gasped.

"Look 'ere," said Mr. Dodds, with ominous quietness, "when you've done your little game."

"It's gone," said Harry in a scared voice; "somebody's taken it."

"Look 'ere, 'Arry, give 'im his money," said Steve impatiently; "a joke's a joke, but we don't want too much of it."

"I ain't got it," said Harry, trembling. "Sure as I stand 'ere it's gone. I took it out of your pocket, and put it under my piller. You saw me, didn't you, Steve?"

"Yes, and I told you not to," said Steve. "Let this be a warning to you not to try and teach lessons to people wot don't want 'em."

"I'm going to the police-station to give 'im in charge," said Mr. Dodds fiercely; "that's wot I'm goin' to do."

"For the Lord's sake don't do that, Sam," said Pilchard, clutching him by the coat.

"'Arry ain't made away with it, Sam," said Steve. "I saw somebody take it out of his bunk while he was asleep."

"Why didn't you stop him?" cried Harry, starting up.

"I didn't like to interfere," said Steve simply; "but I saw where he went to."

"Where?" demanded Mr. Dodds wildly. "Where?"

"He went straight up on deck," said Steve slowly, "walked aft, and then down into the cabin. The skipper woke up, and I heard 'im say something to him."

"Say something to 'im?" repeated the bewildered Dodds. "Wot was it?"

"Well, I 'ardly like to repeat it," said Steve, hesitating.

"Wot was it?" roared the overwrought Mr. Dodds.

"Well, I 'eard this chap say something," said Steve slowly, "and then I heard the skipper's voice. But I don't like to repeat wot 'e said, I reely don't."

"Wot was it?" roared Mr. Dodds, approaching him with clenched fist.

"Well, if you will have it," said Steve, with a little cough, "the old man said to me, 'Well done, Steve,' he ses, 'you're the only sensible man of the whole bilin' lot. Sam's a fool,' 'e ses, 'and 'Arrys worse, an' if it wasn't for men like you, Steve, life wouldn't be worth living.' The skipper's got it now, Sam, and 'e's goin' to give it to your wife to take care of as soon as we get home."

THE MONEY-BOX

Sailormen are not good 'ands at saving money as a rule, said the night-watchman, as he wistfully toyed with a bad shilling on his watch-chain, though to 'ear 'em talk of saving when they're at sea and there isn't a pub within a thousand miles of 'em, you might think different.

It ain't for the want of trying either with some of 'em, and I've known men do all sorts o' things as soon as they was paid off, with a view to saving. I knew one man as used to keep all but a shilling or two in a belt next to 'is skin so that he couldn't get at it easy, but it was all no good. He was always running short in the most inconvenient places. I've seen 'im wriggle for five minutes right off, with a tramcar conductor standing over 'im and the other people in the tram reading their papers with one eye and watching him with the other.

Ginger Dick and Peter Russet—two men I've spoke of to you afore—tried to save their money once. They'd got so sick and tired of spending it all in p'r'aps a week or ten days arter coming ashore, and 'aving to go to sea agin sooner than they 'ad intended, that they determined some way or other to 'ave things different.

They was homeward bound on a steamer from Melbourne when they made their minds up; and Isaac Lunn, the oldest fireman aboard—a very steady old teetotaler—gave them a lot of good advice about it. They all wanted to rejoin the ship when she sailed agin, and 'e offered to take a room ashore with them and mind their money, giving 'em what 'e called a moderate amount each day.

They would ha' laughed at any other man, but they knew that old Isaac was as honest as could be and that their money would be safe with 'im, and at last, after a lot of palaver, they wrote out a paper saying as they were willing for 'im to 'ave their money and give it to 'em bit by bit, till they went to sea agin.

Anybody but Ginger Dick and Peter Russet or a fool would ha' known better than to do such a thing, but old Isaac 'ad got such a oily tongue and seemed so fair-minded about wot 'e called moderate drinking that they never thought wot they was letting themselves in for, and when they took their pay—close on sixteen pounds each—they put the odd change in their pockets and 'anded the rest over to him.

The first day they was as pleased as Punch. Old Isaac got a nice, respectable bedroom for them all, and arter they'd 'ad a few drinks they humoured 'im by 'aving a nice 'ot cup o' tea, and then goin' off with 'im to see a magic-lantern performance.

It was called "The Drunkard's Downfall," and it begun with a young man going into a nice-looking pub and being served by a nice-looking barmaid with a glass of ale. Then it got on to 'arf pints and pints in the next picture, and arter Ginger 'ad seen the lost young man put away six pints in about 'arf a minute, 'e got such a raging thirst on 'im that 'e couldn't sit still, and 'e whispered to Peter Russet to go out with 'im.

"You'll lose the best of it if you go now," ses old Isaac, in a whisper; "in the next picture there's little frogs and devils sitting on the edge of the pot as 'e goes to drink."

"Ginger Dick got up and nodded to Peter."

"Arter that 'e kills 'is mother with a razor," ses old Isaac, pleading with 'im and 'olding on to 'is coat.

Ginger Dick sat down agin, and when the murder was over 'e said it made 'im feel faint, and 'im and Peter Russet went out for a breath of fresh air. They 'ad three at the first place, and then they moved on to another and forgot all about Isaac and the dissolving views until ten o'clock, when Ginger, who 'ad been very liberal to some friends 'e'd made in a pub, found 'e'd spent 'is last penny.

"This comes o' listening to a parcel o' teetotalers," 'e ses, very cross, when 'e found that Peter 'ad spent all 'is money too. "Here we are just beginning the evening and not a farthing in our pockets."

They went off 'ome in a very bad temper. Old Isaac was asleep in 'is bed, and when they woke 'im up and said that they was going to take charge of their money themselves 'e kept dropping off to sleep agin and snoring that 'ard they could scarcely hear themselves speak. Then Peter tipped Ginger a wink and pointed to Isaac's trousers, which were 'anging over the foot of the bed.

Ginger Dick smiled and took 'em up softly, and Peter Russet smiled too; but 'e wasn't best pleased to see old Isaac a-smiling in 'is sleep, as though 'e was 'aving amusing dreams. All Ginger found was a ha'-penny, a bunch o' keys, and a cough lozenge. In the coat and waistcoat 'e found a few tracks folded up, a broken pen-knife, a ball of string, and some other rubbish. Then 'e set down on the foot o' their bed and made eyes over at Peter.

"Wake 'im up agin," ses Peter, in a temper.

Ginger Dick got up and, leaning over the bed, took old Isaac by the shoulders and shook 'im as if 'e'd been a bottle o' medicine.

"Time to get up, lads?" ses old Isaac, putting one leg out o' bed.

"No, it ain't," ses Ginger, very rough; "we ain't been to bed yet. We want our money back."

Isaac drew 'is leg back into bed agin. "Goo' night," he ses, and fell fast asleep.

"He's shamming, that's wot 'e is," ses Peter Russet. "Let's look for it. It must be in the room somewhere."

They turned the room upside down pretty near, and then Ginger Dick struck a match and looked up the chimney, but all 'e found was that it 'adn't been swept for about twenty years, and wot with temper and soot 'e looked so frightful that Peter was arf afraid of 'im.

"I've 'ad enough of this," ses Ginger, running up to the bed and 'olding his sooty fist under old Isaac's nose. "Now, then, where's that money? If you don't give us our money, our 'ard-earned money, inside o' two minutes, I'll break every bone in your body."

"This is wot comes o' trying to do you a favour, Ginger," ses the old man, reproachfully.

"Don't talk to me," ses Ginger, "cos I won't have it. Come on; where is it?"

Old Isaac looked at 'im, and then he gave a sigh and got up and put on 'is boots and 'is trousers.

"I thought I should 'ave a little trouble with you," he ses, slowly, "but I was prepared for that."

"You'll 'ave more if you don't hurry up," ses Ginger, glaring at 'im.

"We don't want to 'urt you, Isaac," ses Peter Russet, "we on'y want our money."

"I know that," ses Isaac; "you keep still, Peter, and see fair-play, and I'll knock you silly arterwards."

He pushed some o' the things into a corner and then 'e spat on 'is 'ands, and began to prance up and down, and duck 'is 'ead about and hit the air in a way that surprised 'em.

"I ain't hit a man for five years," 'e ses, still dancing up and down— "fighting's sinful except in a good cause—but afore I got a new 'art, Ginger, I'd lick three men like you afore breakfast, just to git up a appetite."

"Look, 'ere," ses Ginger; "you're an old man and I don't want to 'urt you; tell us where our money is, our 'ard-earned money, and I won't lay a finger on you."

"I'm taking care of it for you," ses the old man.

Ginger Dick gave a howl and rushed at him, and the next moment Isaac's fist shot out and give 'im a drive that sent 'im spinning across the room until 'e fell in a heap in the fireplace. It was like a kick from a 'orse, and Peter looked very serious as 'e picked 'im up and dusted 'im down.

"You should keep your eye on 'is fist," he ses, sharply.

It was a silly thing to say, seeing that that was just wot 'ad 'appened, and Ginger told 'im wot 'e'd do for 'im when 'e'd finished with Isaac. He went at the old man agin, but 'e never 'ad a chance, and in about three minutes 'e was very glad to let Peter 'elp 'im into bed.

"It's your turn to fight him now, Peter," he ses. "Just move this piller so as I can see."

"Come on, lad," ses the old man.

Peter shook 'is 'ead. "I have no wish to 'urt you, Isaac," he ses, kindly; "excitement like fighting is dangerous for an old man. Give us our money and we'll say no more about it."

"No, my lads," ses Isaac. "I've undertook to take charge o' this money and I'm going to do it; and I 'ope that when we all sign on aboard the Planet there'll be a matter o' twelve pounds each left. Now, I don't want to be 'arsh with you, but I'm going back to bed, and if I 'ave to get up and dress agin you'll wish yourselves dead."

He went back to bed agin, and Peter, taking no notice of Ginger Dick, who kept calling 'im a coward, got into bed alongside of Ginger and fell fast asleep.

They all 'ad breakfast in a coffee-shop next morning, and arter it was over Ginger, who 'adn't spoke a word till then, said that 'e and Peter Russet wanted a little money to go on with. He said they preferred to get their meals alone, as Isaac's face took their appetite away.

"Very good," ses the old man. "I don't want to force my company on nobody," and after thinking 'ard for a minute or two he put 'is 'and in 'is trouser-pocket and gave them eighteen-pence each.

"Wot's this for?" ses Ginger, staring at the money. "Matches?"

"That's your day's allowance," ses Isaac, "and it's plenty. There's ninepence for your dinner, fourpence for your tea, and twopence for a crust o' bread and cheese for supper. And if you must go and drown yourselves in beer, that leaves threepence each to go and do it with."

Ginger tried to speak to 'im, but 'is feelings was too much for 'im, and 'e couldn't. Then Peter Russet swallered something 'e was going to say and asked old Isaac very perlite to make it a quid for 'im because he was going down to Colchester to see 'is mother, and 'e didn't want to go empty-'anded.

"You're a good son, Peter," ses old Isaac, "and I wish there was more like you. I'll come down with you, if you like; I've got nothing to do."

Peter said it was very kind of 'im, but 'e'd sooner go alone, owing to his mother being very shy afore strangers.

"Well, I'll come down to the station and take a ticket for you," ses Isaac.

Then Peter lost 'is temper altogether, and banged 'is fist on the table and smashed 'arf the crockery. He asked Isaac whether 'e thought 'im and Ginger Dick was a couple o' children, and 'e said if 'e didn't give 'em all their money right away 'e'd give 'im in charge to the first policeman they met.

"I'm afraid you didn't intend for to go and see your mother, Peter," ses the old man.

"Look 'ere," ses Peter, "are you going to give us that money?"

"Not if you went down on your bended knees," ses the old man.

"Very good," says Peter, getting up and walking outside; "then come along o' me to find a police-man."

"I'm agreeable," ses Isaac, "but I've got the paper you signed."

Peter said 'e didn't care twopence if 'e'd got fifty papers, and they walked along looking for a police-man, which was a very unusual thing for them to do.

"I 'ope for your sakes it won't be the same police-man that you and Ginger Dick set on in Gun Alley the night afore you shipped on the Planet," ses Isaac, pursing up 'is lips.

"'Tain't likely to be," ses Peter, beginning to wish 'e 'adn't been so free with 'is tongue.

"Still, if I tell 'im, I dessay he'll soon find 'im," ses Isaac; "there's one coming along now, Peter; shall I stop 'im?"

Peter Russet looked at 'im and then he looked at Ginger, and they walked by grinding their teeth. They stuck to Isaac all day, trying to get their money out of 'im, and the names they called 'im was a surprise even to themselves. And at night they turned the room topsy-turvy agin looking for their money and 'ad more unpleasantness when they wanted Isaac to get up and let 'em search the bed.

They 'ad breakfast together agin next morning and Ginger tried another tack. He spoke quite nice to Isaac, and 'ad three large cups o' tea to show 'im 'ow 'e was beginning to like it, and when the old man gave 'em their eighteen-pences 'e smiled and said 'e'd like a few shillings extra that day.

"It'll be all right, Isaac," he ses. "I wouldn't 'ave a drink if you asked me to. Don't seem to care for it now. I was saying so to you on'y last night, wasn't I, Peter?"

"You was," ses Peter; "so was I."

"Then I've done you good, Ginger," ses Isaac, clapping 'im on the back.

"You 'ave," ses Ginger, speaking between his teeth, "and I thank you for it. I don't want drink; but I thought o' going to a music-'all this evening."

"Going to wot?" ses old Isaac, drawing 'imself up and looking very shocked.

"A music-'all," ses Ginger, trying to keep 'is temper.

"A music-'all," ses Isaac; "why, it's worse than a pub, Ginger. I should be a very poor friend o' yours if I let you go there—I couldn't think of it."

"Wot's it got to do with you, you gray-whiskered serpent?" screams Ginger, arf mad with rage. "Why don't you leave us alone? Why don't you mind your own business? It's our money."

Isaac tried to talk to 'im, but 'e wouldn't listen, and he made such a fuss that at last the coffee-shop keeper told 'im to go outside. Peter follered 'im out, and being very upset they went and spent their day's allowance in the first hour, and then they walked about the streets quarrelling as to the death they'd like old Isaac to 'ave when 'is time came.

They went back to their lodgings at dinner-time; but there was no sign of the old man, and, being 'ungry and thirsty, they took all their spare clothes to a pawnbroker and got enough money to go on with. Just to show their independence they went to two music-'ails, and with a sort of idea that they was doing Isaac a bad turn they spent every farthing afore they got 'ome, and sat up in bed telling 'im about the spree they'd 'ad.

At five o'clock in the morning Peter woke up and saw, to 'is surprise, that Ginger Dick was dressed and carefully folding up old Isaac's clothes. At first 'e thought that Ginger 'ad gone mad, taking care of the old man's things like that, but afore 'e could speak Ginger noticed that 'e was awake, and stepped over to 'im and whispered to 'im to dress without making a noise. Peter did as 'e was told, and, more puzzled than ever, saw Ginger make up all the old man's clothes in a bundle and creep out of the room on tiptoe.

"Going to 'ide 'is clothes?" 'e ses.

"Yes," ses Ginger, leading the way downstairs; "in a pawnshop. We'll make the old man pay for to-day's amusements."

Then Peter see the joke and 'e begun to laugh so 'ard that Ginger 'ad to threaten to knock 'is head off to quiet 'im. Ginger laughed 'imself when they got outside, and at last, arter walking about till the shops opened, they got into a pawnbroker's and put old Isaac's clothes up for fifteen shillings.

First thing they did was to 'ave a good breakfast, and after that they came out smiling all over and began to spend a 'appy day. Ginger was in tip-top spirits and so was Peter, and the idea that old Isaac was in bed while they was drinking 'is clothes pleased them more than anything. Twice that evening policemen spoke to Ginger for dancing on the pavement, and by the time the money was spent it took Peter all 'is time to get 'im 'ome.

Old Isaac was in bed when they got there, and the temper 'e was in was shocking; but Ginger sat on 'is bed and smiled at 'im as if 'e was saying compliments to 'im.

"Where's my clothes?" ses the old man, shaking 'is fist at the two of 'em.

Ginger smiled at 'im; then 'e shut 'is eyes and dropped off to sleep.

"Where's my clothes?" ses Isaac, turning to Peter. "Closhe?" ses Peter, staring at 'im.

"Where are they?" ses Isaac.

It was a long time afore Peter could understand wot 'e meant, but as soon as 'e did 'e started to look for 'em. Drink takes people in different ways, and the way it always took Peter was to make 'im one o' the most obliging men that ever lived. He spent arf the night crawling about on all fours looking for the clothes, and four or five times old Isaac woke up from dreams of earthquakes to find Peter 'ad got jammed under 'is bed, and was wondering what 'ad 'appened to 'im.

None of 'em was in the best o' tempers when they woke up next morning, and Ginger 'ad 'ardly got 'is eyes open before Isaac was asking 'im about 'is clothes agin.

"Don't bother me about your clothes," ses Ginger; "talk about something else for a change."

"Where are they?" ses Isaac, sitting on the edge of 'is bed.

Ginger yawned and felt in 'is waistcoat pocket—for neither of 'em 'ad undressed—and then 'e took the pawn-ticket out and threw it on the floor. Isaac picked it up, and then 'e began to dance about the room as if 'e'd gone mad.

"Do you mean to tell me you've pawned my clothes?" he shouts.

"Me and Peter did," ses Ginger, sitting up in bed and getting ready for a row.

Isaac dropped on the bed agin all of a 'cap. "And wot am I to do?" he ses.

"If you be'ave yourself," ses Ginger, "and give us our money, me and Peter'll go and get 'em out agin. When we've 'ad breakfast, that is. There's no hurry."

"But I 'aven't got the money," ses Isaac; "it was all sewn up in the lining of the coat. I've on'y got about five shillings. You've made a nice mess of it, Ginger, you 'ave."

"You're a silly fool, Ginger, that's wot you are," ses Peter.

"Sewn up in the lining of the coat?" ses Ginger, staring.

"The bank-notes was," ses Isaac, "and three pounds in gold 'idden in the cap. Did you pawn that too?"

Ginger got up in 'is excitement and walked up and down the room. "We must go and get 'em out at once," he ses.

"And where's the money to do it with?" ses Peter.

Ginger 'adn't thought of that, and it struck 'im all of a heap. None of 'em seemed to be able to think of a way of getting the other ten shillings wot was wanted, and Ginger was so upset that 'e took no notice of the things Peter kept saying to 'im.

"Let's go and ask to see 'em, and say we left a railway-ticket in the pocket," ses Peter.

Isaac shook 'is 'ead. "There's on'y one way to do it," he ses. "We shall 'ave to pawn your clothes, Ginger, to get mine out with."

"That's the on'y way, Ginger," ses Peter, brightening up. "Now, wot's the good o' carrying on like that? It's no worse for you to be without your clothes for a little while than it was for pore old Isaac."

It took 'em quite arf an hour afore they could get Ginger to see it. First of all 'e wanted Peter's clothes to be took instead of 'is, and when Peter pointed out that they was too shabby to fetch ten shillings 'e 'ad a lot o' nasty things to say about wearing such old rags, and at last, in a terrible temper, 'e took 'is clothes off and pitched 'em in a 'eap on the floor.

"If you ain't back in arf an hour, Peter," 'e ses, scowling at 'im, "you'll 'ear from me, I can tell you."

"Don't you worry about that," ses Isaac, with a smile. "I'm going to take 'em."

"You?" ses Ginger; "but you can't. You ain't got no clothes."

"I'm going to wear Peter's," ses Isaac, with a smile.

Peter asked 'im to listen to reason, but it was all no good. He'd got the pawn-ticket, and at last Peter, forgetting all he'd said to Ginger Dick about using bad langwidge, took 'is clothes off, one by one, and dashed 'em on the floor, and told Isaac some of the things 'e thought of 'im.

The old man didn't take any notice of 'im. He dressed 'imself up very slow and careful in Peter's clothes, and then 'e drove 'em nearly crazy by wasting time making 'is bed.

"Be as quick as you can, Isaac," ses Ginger, at last; "think of us two a-sitting 'ere waiting for you."

"I sha'n't forget it," ses Isaac, and 'e came back to the door after 'e'd gone arf-way down the stairs to ask 'em not to go out on the drink while 'e was away.

It was nine o'clock when he went, and at ha'-past nine Ginger began to get impatient and wondered wot 'ad 'appened to 'im, and when ten o'clock came and no Isaac they was both leaning out of the winder with blankets over their shoulders looking up the road. By eleven o'clock Peter was in very low spirits and Ginger was so mad 'e was afraid to speak to 'im.

They spent the rest o' that day 'anging out of the winder, but it was not till ha'-past four in the afternoon that Isaac, still wearing Peter's clothes and carrying a couple of large green plants under 'is arm, turned into the road, and from the way 'e was smiling they thought it must be all right.

"Wot 'ave you been such a long time for?" ses Ginger, in a low, fierce voice, as Isaac stopped underneath the winder and nodded up to 'em.

"I met a old friend," ses Isaac.

"Met a old friend?" ses Ginger, in a passion. "Wot d'ye mean, wasting time like that while we was sitting up 'ere waiting and starving?"

"I 'adn't seen 'im for years," ses Isaac, "and time slipped away afore I noticed it."

"I dessay," ses Ginger, in a bitter voice. "Well, is the money all right?"

"I don't know," ses Isaac; "I ain't got the clothes."

"Wot?" ses Ginger, nearly falling out of the winder. "Well, wot 'ave you done with mine, then? Where are they? Come upstairs."

"I won't come upstairs, Ginger," ses Isaac, "because I'm not quite sure whether I've done right. But I'm not used to going into pawnshops, and I walked about trying to make up my mind to go in and couldn't."

"Well, wot did you do then?" ses Ginger, 'ardly able to contain hisself.

"While I was trying to make up my mind," ses old Isaac, "I see a man with a barrer of lovely plants. 'E wasn't asking money for 'em, only old clothes."

"Old clothes?" ses Ginger, in a voice as if 'e was being suffocated.

"I thought they'd be a bit o' green for you to look at," ses the old man, 'olding the plants up; "there's no knowing 'ow long you'll be up there. The big one is yours, Ginger, and the other is for Peter."

"'Ave you gone mad, Isaac?" ses Peter, in a trembling voice, arter Ginger 'ad tried to speak and couldn't.

Isaac shook 'is 'ead and smiled up at 'em, and then, arter telling Peter to put Ginger's blanket a little more round 'is shoulders, for fear 'e should catch cold, 'e said 'e'd ask the landlady to send 'em up some bread and butter and a cup o' tea.

They 'eard 'im talking to the landlady at the door, and then 'e went off in a hurry without looking behind 'im, and the landlady walked up and down on the other side of the road with 'er apron stuffed in 'er mouth, pretending to be looking at 'er chimney-pots.

Isaac didn't turn up at all that night, and by next morning those two unfortunate men see 'ow they'd been done. It was quite plain to them that Isaac 'ad been deceiving them, and Peter was pretty certain that 'e took the money out of the bed while 'e was fussing about making it. Old Isaac kept 'em there for three days, sending 'em in their clothes bit by bit and two shillings a day to live on; but they didn't set eyes on 'im agin until they all signed on aboard the Planet, and they didn't set eyes on their money until they was two miles below Gravesend.

W.W. Jacobs – A Short Biography

William Wymark Jacobs was born on September 8, 1863 in the Wapping district of London, England. An author, humorist and dramatist, Jacobs is best remembered for the enduring classic tale of horror - "The Monkey's Paw".

As a youth, Jacobs grew up near the Wapping docks in London, where his father was a wharf manager. The family's first home was home was a house on a River Thames wharf.

The docklands setting would show up frequently in his later literary output. Jacobs, the wharf rat, and his three siblings lost their mother when they were all still young children. Their father, William Gage Jacobs, remarried and fathered a further seven children with his erstwhile housekeeper Ellen Florey. Although he grew up surrounded by poverty, Jacobs himself received a formal education in London, first at a private prep school and later at the Birkbeck Literary and Scientific Institute (now part of the University of London and known as Birkbeck College).

Jacobs' adult working life began with a clerical position at the Post Office Savings Bank. The job was not a stimulating one but Jacobs put his imagination to good use and started to write short stories, sketches and articles, many of which appeared in the Post Office house publication "Blackfriars Magazine."

Although Jacobs did receive his fair share of rejection slips at the beginning of his career, many works written during this period of clerical employment appeared in the "Idler" and "Today" magazines, both of which were edited by noted humorist Jerome K. Jerome, who had taken a liking to Jacobs' stories.

From 1898, Jacobs also published stories in "The Strand", a popular, monthly fiction and general interest magazine. The arrangement stayed in place for most of his life and many of the works in Jacobs' subsequent collections – including the nautical serialization A Master of Craft (1899-1900) - appeared there first.

Jacobs' first volume of collected works was published in 1896. Many Cargoes, a selection of sea-faring yarns, established Jacobs as a popular writer and humorist with a penchant for authentic dialogue and trick endings (critics of the day referred to him as the "O. Henry of the Waterfront").

A year later he published a novelette, The Skipper's Wooing, and in 1898 and another collection of short stories titled Sea Urchins. These works painted vivid, if imaginatively stretched, pictures of dockland and seafaring London with colourful characters (such as "The Night Watchman", Ginger Dick) that now seem archetypal.

Many of Jacobs' periodical publications and first editions were illustrated with woodcuts and ink drawings, as was still the custom at the turn of the 20th century. The author worked regularly with artists such as E.W. Kemble, who had illustrated Mark Twain's Adventures of Huckleberry Finn and Harriet Beecher Stowe's Uncle Tom's Cabin, and his good friend Will Owen, who eventually became a household name on the strength of his iconic Bisto Kids, Bovril and Lux Soap advertising posters.

By 1899, Jacobs was able to quit the post office and finally begin a career making a living as a full-time writer.

He married the noted suffragist Agnes Eleanor Williams (who had been jailed for her protest activities) in 1900. They set up a household in Loughton, Essex as well as living part of the year in central London. The couple went on to have five children together though their marriage was considered an unhappy one.

The publication of two short novels: At Sunwich Port (a romantic tale of rival sea captains in the fictional seaside community of Sunwich standing in for the actual East England community of Sandwich, Kent) and Dialstone Lane (another small town romance involving intrigue and buried treasure), in 1902 and 1904 respectively, cemented Jacobs' reputation as one of the leading British authors of the new century.

On the foundations of a continuing ability to write for his audience he was readily published though he never strayed too far from what was becoming his familiar, dependable style. There followed a string of further successful publications, including Captain's All (1905), Night Watches (1914), The Castaways (1916), and Sea Whispers (1926). Jacobs published eighteen books in all during his lifetime, thirteen collections and five novels.

As a storyteller, Jacobs is perhaps better remembered for a handful of brief tales of the supernatural than for his popular nautical-themed works. The most famous of these, The Monkey's Paw, originally appeared as part of the 1902 short story collection The Lady of the Barge. It is an economically written story about a shriveled talisman, a monkey's paw that brings grief and horror in the wake of all too literal wish granting. The story has been adapted for other media repeatedly, starting with a one-act play performed at London's Haymarket Theatre in 1903. There have been multiple film adaptations of the story in the modern era; some of us are familiar with its appearance in an episode of the popular animated series, The Simpsons.

Another macabre gem, The Toll-House, was published as part of the collection Sailor's Knots in 1909. Jacob's once again employs a sparse style to tell the story of a group of men who spend the night in a famously haunted house on a dare (a noticeably similar narrative concept was put to use in the much earlier play The Ghost of Jerry Bundler, which had launched Jacobs' parallel career as a dramatist back in 1899 when it was produced at the St. James Theatre in London). Innovative at the time of writing, these sparingly written, atmospheric ghost stories are now familiar classics of the supernatural genre.

Though prolific in his younger years, Jacobs' productivity dropped dramatically after the start of World War I. Yet even in self-imposed semi-retirement Jacobs was still recognized as a leading humorist, ranked alongside such writers as P. G. Wodehouse and George Birmingham. He enjoyed continuing influence and elevated status among his fellow writers as evidenced by these comments attributed to his colleague Henry James:

"Mr. Jacobs, I envy you. You are popular! Your admirable work is appreciated by a wide circle of readers; it has achieved popularity. Mine never goes into a second edition."

James' literary fortunes would, of course, change, but his back-handedly complimentary admiration is compelling evidence of Jacobs' reputation as a writer and humourist both for his audience and his perhaps more admired literary colleagues.

Though Jacobs would create little in the way of new work after 1911, he was still writing. In these later years, seemingly burnt out creatively, Jacobs concentrated more on writing dramatizations and adaptations of his existing stories, including Beauty and the Barge (a film version starring Margaret Rutherford was also released in 1937) and In the Dark (a one act play that is often performed pr published with The Monkey's Paw adaptation).

Though admired by loyal readers throughout his lifetime, Jacobs has been almost completely forgotten since. Critics are at a loss to name a single reason why - Jacobs is universally considered to be a fine and imaginative literary craftsman. But, as critic John Wain suggested in a 1960 essay, perhaps Jacobs' humour may have been too gentle to persist into the cruel and sarcastic modern era, his dry pokes at proletariat hardship no longer suiting the times.

Nonetheless, Jacobs' legacy remains solid: he continued Dickens' (a writer with whom he is also often compared) tradition for sharing working class stories in authentic vernacular. And polished narratives such as The Monkey's Paw set a standard for the clever use of horror in fiction and popular culture that endures to this day. Indeed recently his works have begun to show an increased demand and appreciation in a world that is constantly looking over its shoulder.

William Wymark Jacobs died in a North London nursing home in Hornsey Lane, Islington on September 1st, 1943, just a week before his 80th birthday.

W.W. Jacobs – A Concise Bibliography

NOVELS AND SHORT STORY COLLECTIONS
MANY CARGOES (SHORT STORIES) (1896)
THE SKIPPER'S WOOING (1897)
SEA URCHINS (SHORT STORIES) (1898) aka MORE CARGOES
A MASTER OF CRAFT (1900)
LIGHT FREIGHTS (SHORT STORIES) (1901)
THE LADY OF THE BARGE (SHORT STORIES) (1902)
AT SUNWICH PORT (1902)
DIALSTONE LANE (1902)
SALTHAVEN (1908)
CAPTAINS ALL (SHORT STORIES) (1911)
NIGHT WATCHERS (SHORT STORIES) (1914)
DEEP WATERS (SHORT STORIES) (1919)

SHORT STORIES (INCLUDING THOSE USED IN THE COLLECTIONS ABOVE)
A BENEFIT PERFORMANCE
A BLACK AFFAIR
A CASE OF DESERTION
A CHANGE OF TREATMENT
A CIRCULAR TOUR
A DISCIPLINARIAN
A DISTANT RELATIVE
A GARDEN PLOT
A GOLDEN VENTURE
A HARBOUR OF REFUGE
A LOVE KNOT
A LOVE PASSAGE
A MARKED MAN
A MIXED PROPOSAL
A RASH EXPERIMENT
A SAFETY MATCH
A SPIRIT OF AVARICE
A TIGER'S SKIN
ADMIRAL PETERS
AFTER THE INQUEST
ALF'S DREAM
AN ADULTERATION ACT
AN ELABORATE ELOPEMENT
AN INTERVENTION
AN ODD FREAK

ANGELS' VISITS
BACK TO BACK
BEDRIDDEN
THE WINTER OFFENSIVE
THE BEQUEST
BILL'S LAPSE
BILL'S PAPER CHASE
BLUNDELL'S IMPROVEMENT
THE BOATSWAIN'S WATCH
THE BOATSWAIN'S MATE
BOB'S REDEMPTION
BREAKING A SPELL
BREVET RANK
BROTHER HUTCHINS
THE BULLY OF THE "CAVENDISH"
THE CABIN PASSENGER
CAPTAIN ROGERS
THE CAPTAIN'S EXPLOIT
CAPTAINS ALL
THE CASTAWAY
THE CHANGELING
"CHOICE SPIRITS"
THE CONSTABLE'S MOVE
CONTRABAND OF WAR
THE CONVERT
THE COOK OF THE "GANNET"
CUPBOARD LOVE
DESERTED
DIRTY WORK
THE DISBURSEMENT SHEET
DIXON'S RETURN
DOUBLE DEALING
THE DREAMER
DUAL CONTROL
EASY MONEY
ESTABLISHING RELATIONS
FAIRY GOLD
FALSE COLOURS
FAMILY CARES
FINE FEATHERS
FOR BETTER OR WORSE
THE FOUR PIGEONS
FRIENDS IN NEED
GOOD INTENTIONS
THE GREY PARROT
THE GUARDIAN ANGEL
THE HEAD OF THE FAMILY
HER UNCLE
HIS LORDSHIP
HIS OTHER SELF
HOMEWARD BOUND

HUSBANDRY
IN BORROWED PLUMES
IN LIMEHOUSE REACH
IN MID-ATLANTIC
IN THE FAMILY
IN THE LIBRARY
JERRY BUNDLER
KEEPING UP APPEARANCES
KEEPING WATCH
THE LADY OF THE BARGE
LAWYER QUINCE
THE LOST SHIP
LOW WATER
MADE TO MEASURE
THE MADNESS OF MR. LISTER
"MANNERS MAKYTH MAN"
MATED
"MATRIMONIAL OPENINGS"
MIXED RELATIONS
MONEY CHANGERS
THE MONEY-BOX
THE MONKEY'S PAW
MRS. BUNKER'S CHAPERON
THE NEST EGG
ODD MAN OUT
THE OLD MAN OF THE SEA
OUTSAILED
OVER THE SIDE
PAYING OFF
THE PERSECUTION OF BOB PRETTY
PETER'S PENCE
PICKLED HERRING
PRIVATE CLOTHES
PRIZE MONEY
THE RESURRECTION OF MR. WIGGETT
THE RIVAL BEAUTIES
RULE OF THREE
SAM'S BOY
SAM'S GHOST
SELF-HELP
SENTENCE DEFERRED
SHAREHOLDERS
SKILLED ASSISTANCE
THE SKIPPER OF THE "OSPREY"
SMOKED SKIPPER
STEPPING BACKWARDS
STRIKING HARD
THE SUBSTITUTE
THE TEMPTATION OF SAMUEL BURGE
THE TEST
THE THREE SISTERS

TO HAVE AND TO HOLD
"THE TOLL-HOUSE"
TWIN SPIRITS
TWO OF A TRADE
THE UNDERSTUDY
THE UNKNOWN
THE VIGIL
WATCH-DOGS
THE WEAKER VESSEL
THE WELL
THE WHITE CAT

STAGE
THE GHOST OF JERRY BUNDLER (1899) (In London)

FILM ADAPTATIONS
A MASTER OF CRAFT (1922)
THE MONKEY'S PAW (1933)
OUR RELATIONS, a Laurel & Hardy film, "suggested by" to Jacobs' "The Money Box." (1936)
FOOTSTEPS IN THE FOG, from the short story The Interruption. (1955)